RUINING HIM

BOOK 2, MCKINLEY RANCH DUET

KYLIE KENT

MCCARTNEY INDUSTRIES

RUINING HIM

THE MCKINLEY RANCH DUET

Book 2

Kylie Kent

Social Media:
Website & Newsletter: www.kyliekent.com
Facebook: @kyliekent2020
Instagram Follow: @author_kylie_kent_

Ebook ISBN 13: 978-0-6489981-8-1

Paperback ISBN 13: 9780648998198

Cover Illustration by
Kate Farlow - Y'all that graphic
Editing services provided by
Kat Pagan – https://www.facebook.com/PaganProofreading

This book contains scenes and discussions of non-consensual sexual acts, profanity, sexual content and violence. If any of these are triggers for you, you should consider skipping this read. This is book 2 in a 2-part duet; expect NO cliff-hanger.

This is a work of fiction. Names, characters, businesses, places, events and incidents are either the products of the author's imagination or used in a fictitious manner. Any resemblance to actual persons, living or dead, or actual events is purely coincidental.

This book is dedicated to all the survivors. All who live with the internal and external scars left behind. Never stop fighting for you, never give up on finding your happily ever after.

BLURB

Josh

Emily came crashing back into my life, bringing with her everything I was missing.

But she's not the same girl I knew years ago. Gone is the girl who was always happy and eager to please everyone. The one who didn't let life get her down.

She's conquered her demons but they still haunt her whenever she closes her eyes. Her screams tear through the darkness night after night.

She thinks she needs to get away, to keep running. To leave me behind.

But I won't lose her again; I will slay anything, *anyone,* who thinks they can get in the way of my keeping her.

Emily

I wasn't meant to let myself get attached to Josh again. I wasn't meant to stay this long.

Now he knows my biggest secret; he knows I'm not the sweet girl he thinks I am.

I'm being chased, hunted down like prey.

But I won't let my past mistakes hurt Josh.

I need to leave before *he* finds me.

Leaving Josh behind is not going to be as easy as I thought it would be, but it's my only option. I'll do whatever it is I have to do to protect him, even if that means I have to ***Ruin Him***.

CHAPTER 1

JOSH

Theme song - Ruining Me, Danni Giddings

Married, she's fucking married. Or *was* married. How the fuck did I not know that? Why do I feel like my heart just fucking shattered into a million pieces? That should have been me, only me. She went and married someone who wasn't fucking me.

"Fuck!" I yell, pulling at my hair.

"Josh, just stop the car. Let me out," Emily whispers while moving as far away from me as she can get.

I look at her, really look at her. She's scared. I don't think I've really ever seen her this scared before. I need to calm down; my yelling is not helping her at all. But fuck, she fucking married someone else.

"I can't." My voice is hoarse, the words barely audible.

"*You* don't need to. Just tell him to stop the car and let me out."

"I can't let you go, Emmy. I'm never going to be able to let you go. You knew that before you came back. I warned you if you came back, I'd be keeping you."

"You have to let me go. You don't understand… They're going to find me, and I'd rather not drag you down with my mess."

"Your mess is my mess, Emmy. I'll fix this. I can fix this."

Emmy shakes her head no. She doesn't say anything, just looks down at her hands and continues to shake her head no repeatedly.

"Tell me why?" I ask. I need to know why she fucking married someone else.

"You want me to tell you why I killed him? I was cooking dinner; it was his favourite. I thought he'd be in a good mood because he liked when I cooked spaghetti. When I heard the door jingle, I ran into the bedroom to check the bed, then to the bathroom and redid the towels. By the time I got back out to the kitchen, the sauce was burning."

Emmy hesitates and stares at me, silently begging me to tell her to stop. I probably should. I know I'm not going to like whatever it is she has to fucking say. But fuck, I need to know. When I asked her to tell me why, I was referring to the whole marriage thing. I want to fucking know why the fuck she married him.

I wait her out, not breaking eye contact. I can do this. I can sit here and listen to whatever it is she has to say. I need to do this.

"He… I knew he was going to be mad. I don't know why I did it, but I picked up a small knife out of the block and hid it behind my back. He…" Emmy shakes her head no again.

"He what, Emmy?" I ask her, not moving a muscle. I'm so afraid I'll scare her off and she'll stop talking. This is the most she's ever fucking talked to me about this prick.

"He got mad, threw the sauce. He hit me a few times. I don't know why I did it. I don't know why now. It wasn't different from any other time. But when he was..." She glances at me briefly then looks away. Again, I wait, with the patience of a damn saint.

"When he was raping me, I remembered I had the knife in my hand. I don't know what came over me. I just brought the knife up and jammed it into his neck. There was so much blood. It was everywhere."

"Stop the fucking car now!" I yell at the driver. He's quick to pull over to the side. As soon as I jump out of the vehicle, I'm bent over, throwing my fucking guts up. I watch the black SUV come to a stop behind me, and looking over my shoulder, I see another one just up the road in front a bit.

Paul springs from the SUV at the back with a bottle of water in hand. Fuck me, I've gutted and cut up human bodies like a bloody butcher and never once have I spilled my guts over that. But the image of Emily being beaten, being... *raped*. The thought of her having to endure that for years is too much. I want that fucker's blood. The inferno that's roaring inside me is the most intense I've ever felt.

I'm fucking losing it. Bending over, I'm clutching at my knees, trying to breathe through this. Attempting to calm the fucking beast within. I know I need to be the strong one here. I need to not let Emmy see me fall apart so easily. But fuck me, this is hard.

What's worse? It's all my fucking fault. If I hadn't made her leave town, this would never have happened to her. I'll never be able to forgive myself. How can I expect Emily to forgive me?

"Boss, you all right?" Paul asks, holding out the bottle of water towards me.

I take the bottle and swish some water around my mouth before spitting it out. "No, I'm obviously not fucking good," I grunt out.

"Well, you might want to get over whatever it is real quick. We got company and that girl of yours needs to be out of sight." He nods his head towards Emily, who is standing on the other side of the car, glaring straight at me with an expression I can't read.

"Fuck!" Passing the water bottle back to Paul, I make my way over to Emmy. "Babe, you need to get back in the car."

She just stares at me. I don't like the blank look on her face. Why the fuck can't I read what she's thinking? I've always been able to. It's like she's shut down, closed off all emotions.

"Emmy, get in the fucking car, now." I growl when she makes no effort to move. The moment the sound leaves the back of my throat, I know I fucked up again. I need to remember to be gentler with her. Right now, though, I need to get her back in the car and out of view. I see a black SUV coming up the road before slowing to a stop.

"Fuck, I'm sorry, Emmy. I'll make this up to you later," I whisper as I manhandle her, picking her up and sitting her in the back seat of the car. I make sure I flick the child lock on the door before shutting her in.

Turning around, I see some ass stagger out of the SUV that's just pulled up behind Paul's car. Four of Paul's guys jump out of the vehicle in front of mine, coming to a stand behind me. Paul goes to step forward and I pull him back.

I wait for the ass to speak as he stops directly in front of me, obviously knowing who the fuck I am.

"Mr. McKinley, you're a hard man to track down."

"Depends on who's looking," I reply.

"Detective Jones." He holds out a hand. I look down at his outstretched palm and dismiss it. Like fuck, am I shaking hands with this fucker.

"What can I do for you, detective?" I ask.

"I'm looking for a woman—Emily Livingston. Know anything about her whereabouts?"

"Emily Livingston. I haven't heard that name since high school." I shrug my shoulders. Everything in me wants to end this motherfucker right here. "I heard she left town right after graduation. Why are you looking for her? What'd she do?"

"That's classified, but if you do run into her, here's my card. I'd like to ask her a few questions."

He holds out a card, which I take and pass off to Paul.

"Sure."

I watch as he turns and walks back to his car. "Detective," I yell out before he gets in. Turning back, he raises his eyebrows in question at me.

"I'm curious… how exactly do you plan to question a dead girl?" I smirk, knowing full well this is the asshole who signed both Emily and her mother's death certificates. The smile falls from his face momentarily, shock replacing his confidence.

"My sources tell me Miss Livingston is very much alive and breathing. For now," he says as he climbs into the car. Paul steps in front of me, stopping me in my tracks.

"Do not let him rile you up, Josh. You reacting right now is exactly what that prick wants."

I know he's right, but fuck, I want to gut the fucker. I want to hear his screams as I skin him alive. Nobody will ever threaten Emily and walk away unscathed. He may think he's walking away, but I now know who he is. Before the day is out, I'll make sure I know everything there is to know about Detective Jones.

As soon as the detective drives off, I open the door of the car, instructing the security detail that they are not to leave any room between the convoy. I will not take chances with Emily's safety.

When I get in the car, Emily is sitting on the very far side, scowling in my direction. Fuck, how the fuck am I going to fix this? Reaching across, I pull the seat belt over her shoulder and plug the buckle in. Lingering a little in her space, I inhale her scent.

She always smells so fucking good, like wild berries. "I'm sorry, so fucking sorry, Emmy. I know it's not forgivable, what I've done, but I will try every day to earn your forgiveness."

I sit back on the other side of the car. "We're going to the penthouse," I instruct the driver before pressing the button and winding up the privacy screen. As soon as the divider's up, and it's just Emmy and me, I breathe a sigh of relief. I don't need to pretend with her. I don't need to be anyone other than me.

Leaning over, I grab at my hair as my head hangs down. I breathe in and count to ten, over and over again. I'm trying everything I can to stop myself from reaching for her. She needs to make the first move. The disdain on her face when I got in the car was clear as day.

She hates me. *Rightfully so, too.* I'm a fucking asshole. She's never going to be able to forgive me for what happened to her, the fact that none of that would have happened if I never chased her out of town.

"Josh?" her quiet, timid voice asks.

I look over to see her eyes red, silent tears staining her cheeks. Every time I see her cry, I feel her pain right down to my core. It shatters something in me. As broken as I am, it surprises me that there is anything left to break, but for Emily, there is always more.

I reach a hand up slowly to her face; she doesn't flinch at my touch. It's a small, hollow victory. "I'm sorry," I repeat as I wipe her tears away with my thumb.

"I understand. I won't be a problem for you anymore. Just stop the car and I'll get out," she whispers.

"You're not fucking going anywhere, Emmy. You don't understand. I refuse to lose you again. I won't lose you again. I can't."

"Josh, I'm only going to bring trouble to your life. Just hearing what I did, what I've done, made you sick. How can you even look at me? I can't even look at myself in the mirror without seeing it."

"The only thing I see when I look at you, Emmy, is a fucking angel, my fucking angel. A survivor. When I look at you, I see everything that's good in this world." Fuck me, she thinks I was sick because of what she did. "God, Emily, I wasn't sick because of what you did. What happened to you should never have fucking happened. It's my fault. I should never have made you leave town. If I didn't, then none of that would have happened. I would have been around to protect you."

"No, it's my fault. *I* left town, Josh. *I* made choices that led me to Trent. What he did is not on you. It's on me. I should have been smarter, gotten out of that situation earlier."

"This isn't something we are going to agree on, babe. But know that from here on out, it's me and you. Just the two of us against the world. Nothing will take you away from me, Emmy. I will fix this."

I lean in and claim her lips with mine. Her hands reach up and pull my head in closer to her. She unclasps her seat belt and straddles me, her pussy crashing down hard on my cock. "Fuck, babe, as much as I want you, this isn't safe. You should have a seat belt on."

"Shut up," Emmy growls as her hands rip at my own buckle. Okay, guess we're doing this. Her fingers are frantic as she tries to undo my jeans. I take over for her—thinking there'd be less chance of a zipper injury if I do it myself.

As soon as my zipper is lowered, her palm wraps around my shaft, pumping up and down a few times.

My hands go to her ass as she hovers above me. Moving her panties aside, I line my cock up with her entrance, her pussy sliding down on me like a goddamn glove, pulsing and clenching at my cock.

She stills as she bottoms out. Her head leans back, her mouth open and her eyes closed. I wish I had a camera to capture this look right here. This has to be one of my favourite expressions of hers. Her body shivers as she tilts her head back upright, locking those blue eyes of hers onto mine.

CHAPTER 2

EMILY

Locking eyes with Josh, I try to tell him everything I struggle to say in words. How much I really love him, need him, cherish him. I want to believe in the fantasy he's trying to sell me. That we will get our happily ever after, but no matter how much I try, I just can't see how reality is going to let that happen.

Right now, I can give in to this feeling, this need to have him as close as I can possibly get. I lift my hips and start rocking back and forward. Every time I come back down, my clit hits him right on his pubic bone. The sensations going through me are unbelievable. I was in such a frenzied rush to get him inside me, but now that he's there, I don't want it to end. I want to take my time and drag this out as long as I can.

My hands roam up and under his shirt, over the ridges and grooves of his abs. All I can think of is how much I want to run my tongue along these grooves. I ride him as slowly as I can. Josh's hands squeeze the globes of my ass, his grunts and groans filling the car, but he does nothing to take control of the speed or tempo of my movements.

"Fuck, Em, you were fucking made for me. This pussy was made to ride my cock." Josh growls into my ear as he takes the lobe between his teeth and sucks.

"Mmm, I don't want this feeling to end, Josh."

"This is never going to end, babe," he promises as I pick up my pace again, chasing that bliss that I know will come crashing over me in waves of pleasure. I lean my head back as Josh moves his mouth to the crook of my neck. His teeth gently graze the delicate skin there before he bites down.

The pain of the bite sends jolts of electricity straight to my core, and I explode. My juices flood him as he holds my hips still, riding me through my orgasm and finding his own release.

"You. Are. Mine," he states as he empties himself inside me. I collapse into him, my head falling to his chest, my fingers wrapping around the fabric of his shirt. I'm not ready to let go of this feeling yet.

Josh runs his hands through my hair, laying tender kisses to my forehead. It confuses me how he can be so gentle and loving towards me, yet cold and closed off to everyone else. The way he makes me feel like I'm the most important thing in the world to him is dangerous. I want to keep him. Knowing that I can't is eating me up. I know I'm going to have to let him go eventually. Nothing good lasts forever and this right here, sitting on his lap, being wrapped up in his arms—this is a good feeling.

Shaking the thoughts away, I slip off his lap and slide back into my seat, pulling the seat belt back on. I can't even look at him right now. What the hell is wrong with me? I'm so afraid he's going to be able to see right through me. I can't let him in on the internal struggle I'm currently having about staying.

I know the best thing is for me to disappear. It will ruin him, but in the end, it will also save him. I can't let anyone else go down for the mess I've made. I just need to figure out how to get away from him.

Josh reaches across the car and picks up my hand, entwining his fingers with mine. I can feel his eyes on me as I stare out the window. He's silent. The stroking of his thumb on my wrist is comforting in the strangest way. Just his touch soothes all my aches and pains. Whenever his skin makes contact with mine, it feels like I can breathe again after being held under water.

If I were to ask a shrink, I'm sure I'd be told I was developing an unhealthy, co-dependent relationship with Josh. Even knowing this, I still want him.

"Emmy, whatever you're thinking, stop. I promise it's going to be okay. I will fix this."

"You can't possibly know what I'm thinking, Josh." Annoyed that he reads me so bloody well, I try to pull my hand out of his. He just holds onto it tighter, refusing to let me cut off our connection.

"I know that you've got one foot out the door, ready to run at any given chance."

"I can't let you deal with my mess. I'm a mess, Josh. I have so many issues up here right now. Why the hell would you want me around?" I ask, pointing to my head. He has to understand how damaged I am.

"*You* think you're a mess. I think you're fucking beautiful. *Perfect.* Whatever we have to do to deal with this situation, we will do it together. I won't have it any other way."

"I'm far from perfect. I can't get these images out of my head. I can't close my eyes and not see it, not see what I did."

"*What you did?* Let me tell you what you did,

Emily. What you did was survive. What you did was brave, courageous and fucking amazing. You didn't do anything wrong; you have nothing to feel guilty about. Do you hear me? *You have done nothing wrong,* Emmy. You survived a situation you should never have fucking been put in."

"But that's the thing, Josh. I don't feel guilty. I'm not sorry for what I did. When I close my eyes, I'm not consumed by guilt, but fear. I'm so tired of being scared all the damn time."

Josh unclips his seat belt and moves to the middle of the car, right next to me. He holds my face in his hands, resting his forehead on mine.

"Tell me what you're afraid of most in the world, Emmy. What's your biggest fear?" he asks.

I think about it for a while. I'm scared of the future, of what my future looks like. I'm scared that I didn't kill Trent and he's going to find me again. I'm scared that I'm going to spend the rest of my life behind bars for what I did. But my biggest fear, the thing that terrifies me the most, is Josh.

I close my eyes and confess this realization to him. "You. You're my biggest fear, Josh. I'm so afraid that you're going to wake up one day and decide that you're finished with me again. I'm afraid that you're going to send me away. I'm scared that you won't be able to look at me the same way... now that you know what I did. My biggest fear is losing you... again."

When I open my eyes, I'm met with Josh's blue orbs sucking me into his trance. I can see so many different emotions in his eyes. But the one that stands out the most is love. When he looks at me, I can always see love.

"Emily, I swear on everything that you will never lose me. You are the only person I've ever loved. You are the only person I *will* ever love. I'm sorry that I've made you feel like you didn't always have me, but I promise I've always been yours. Only yours."

"What kind of future do you really think we can have, Josh? I have the police looking for me. I killed someone..." I whisper.

"Babe, I've killed someone on every day that ends with a Y. It's not a big deal. And that cop will not get anywhere near you."

"Why do I feel like you're telling me the truth?"

"Because I always do and always will tell you the truth. Emmy, you watched me shoot someone in our apartment. You've never once questioned me about it or looked at me differently. Why do you think I would love you any less?"

"I know you, Josh, and that's crazy, considering our history. But I know your soul, and it's not bad. I can't answer why what you do to others doesn't bother me. It just doesn't." I shrug.

"Good, because I will stop at nothing to make sure you are safe."

I'M jolted awake as I feel my body being lifted. "Shh, it's okay. I've got you," Josh says. I let my head fall onto his chest momentarily before my brain makes the connection that he's carrying me.

"Wait. I'm awake. Put me down." I wiggle around, which only makes his arms hold me tighter.

"No."

"Josh, don't be ridiculous. Put me down. I can walk. You don't need to carry me."

"I know I don't need to. I want to, so I am."

"Look, I didn't want to say this, but you're making me. You should really take better care with your back; you're not getting any younger. You should probably leave the heavy lifting to the young folk."

"Are you calling me old, Emmy?" He laughs.

"If the shoe fits." I smile up at him.

"You do know we are the same age, right? Also, I'm more than happy to prove to you just how much vitality this body of mine still has."

"We *are* the same age, which is why I know how old you are. I'm pretty sure I saw a grey hair yesterday."

Josh stops abruptly. "Babe, that's not something to joke about. Where was it? It's probably just dust. I am not going grey. There's no fucking way." Shaking his head, he continues walking, pressing the button for the lift with his elbow.

"I meant on me. I saw a grey hair on me, not you. I didn't know you were so vain. Are you really worried about a grey hair?"

"On me, yes. On you, not at all. In fact, I can't wait to see you old and wrinkly with a full head of grey hair."

"That's weird. Do you have a granny fetish I should know about?" Josh laughs as the doors to the lift open and he steps in. Turning back around to face the door, he shifts all of my weight into one arm so he can use his thumbprint to send the lift to the penthouse.

Huh, I wonder if my thumb would do that?

"I don't have a granny fetish. I have an Emmy fetish. Everything Emmy turns me the fuck on. But mostly, I'm looking forward to seeing you old and grey because it will mean we'd have had a whole life together."

"Will we be sitting on rocking chairs next to each other on the porch of an old cabin?"

"We will be doing whatever it is you want to be doing, Em."

"Mmm, well, I think that when we are old, I want to be sitting on a porch in a rocking chair while we watch our grandchildren play in the yard." I don't tell him that I can't see how we can ever have that future—*the dream*. Instead, I do what I'm good at. I pretend. I pretend that Josh and I have a future together, that we will have a soccer team of kids and more grandchildren than we can count.

We'll spend holidays watching the brumbies run free and wild at the cabin we just spent a whole week in. If I had it my way, we'd be going back there. Out in the middle of nowhere, just the two of us. And all the horses of course.

Josh finally lets me down when he walks into the penthouse, holding me until he's sure I have my footing.

Josh looks around the room, his jaw tightening the more his head turns.

"Come on, I think you need to rest," he says, grabbing my hand and tugging me towards the bedroom. With his free arm, he pulls his phone out of his pocket and starts typing on it one-handed.

When we get into the bedroom, he escorts me

straight into the walk-in closet, closing the door behind him. He places his finger up to his lips, indicating for me to keep quiet.

I don't know what's going on. Panic starts to kick in as I take note of Josh's posture, his taut jaw clenched. His eyes stormy blue, a cold, calculating look to them. Yet, I'm not scared of him. He looks like he's ready to pounce on anything that's willing to jump out at him.

I don't understand why he makes me feel so safe. I should be looking for a way out of this closet. Instead, I'm standing here, waiting for his next instruction. If I'm honest with myself though, I'd follow Josh into the pits of Hell if it meant I'd get to stay with him.

CHAPTER 3

JOSH

I'm fucking fuming, trying my hardest not to let the anger inside me take over. Emily does not deserve to see the shit show that would happen if I let this rage seep out. It's burning me up. I can feel my veins heating up and pulsing as the fire tries to engulf me whole.

I need to calm down. She is safe; she is with me. If I let the rage win, if I let her see what happens when this overwhelming anger finds its way to the surface, I have no doubt that it will scare the shit out of her. And that's the last thing I want to do.

She's just starting to show moments of her spark,

her humour and sass. I don't want to do anything that will take that away.

I knew the moment I walked into the penthouse that someone had been there. There were shoe prints on the white marble tiles. The maid service has never left so much as a speck of dust in this place.

The tiny cameras disguised as ornaments were the other tell. Most people probably wouldn't notice an odd ornament on a shelf they barely look at, but I'm not most people. A little OCD? Maybe, but when something's been moved, or in this case, added, I can always spot it. That, and the fact that they were subpar. I could see the tiny red light blinking from a distance.

I counted three, just in the living room. Taking Emmy into the bedroom, I saw another two sitting on the dresser. The fact that someone is watching us, watching her, pisses me the fuck off.

Looking around the closet I've locked us in together, I can't see any more surprises in here. But I'll be damned if I'm letting Emily out until those fucking cameras are gone.

I hold my finger up, indicating for Emily to be quiet. I don't know if those cameras in the bedroom have audio or not.

I've sent a message to Sam. If anyone can come and clean those cameras and find out what IP address they're feeding back to, it's him. He's thirty minutes away though, so I guess Emily and I are going to have to get comfortable in this closet, because I'll be fucked if I'm going to let whatever fucker put those cameras out there get another glimpse of her.

Pulling her to the very back of the closet, I sit on the bench seat that's positioned against the wall before tugging her down onto my lap. She doesn't hesitate, straddling me as she wraps her arms around my neck.

Leaning into her ear, I whisper, "Get comfy, babe. We're going to be staying in here for at least thirty minutes."

She looks at me, so many questions held in her gaze. "Why?" she mouths.

"I don't want you to worry. I promise I will never let anything happen to you. I just noticed some things in the apartment that shouldn't be here—that's all. Sam's on his way over to get rid of them."

"What kind of things, Josh?" Her voice is barely above a whisper.

"Cameras."

Emily's eyebrows draw down as confusion crosses her features. "Why would someone put cameras in your apartment?"

"No idea, but I'm sure as fuck going to find out." I trail kisses up the side of her neck. "In the meantime, how do you suppose we can kill thirty minutes?" I waggle my eyebrows up and down at her, attempting to put her at ease.

"Mmm, well, you could braid my hair?" She smiles.

"You want me to braid your hair?"

"Well, what are my other options here?"

"I could do that thing you like. You know, the one where I use my tongue to paint one of the classics on your pussy."

Emily's hips wiggle slightly, her pussy pressing onto my hardening cock. Just the thought of tasting her is giving me a raging hard-on.

"As much as I like that idea, and believe me I do, I'm not sure I'd be able to stay quiet. Considering we are whispering right now, how would I be able to whisper scream out your name when you make me come?"

She's got a good point. "Okay, hair braiding it is." Standing up, I sit her on the floor and walk over to the opposite side of the wardrobe—the one I've had fitted out for her. The racks are lined with clothes, shoes and accessories; I had Ella help me out in getting this done while I took Emily to the property in Western Australia this past week.

There's a dressing table with stacks of bottles of girly shit. I find a brush and a pack of plastic hair bands. When I turn around, Emily is scowling at me. It's hard not to laugh; she looks so fucking cute.

"What's wrong?" I whisper once I'm seated behind her. Her shoulders are stiff. She shakes her head no.

"Emmy, what's wrong?" I ask again.

"I'm fine. It doesn't matter."

"It matters to me. What's wrong?" She's silent. She doesn't want to tell me. I decide to wait her silence out and start brushing her hair.

After three minutes of combing through her loose curls, her body is still stiff. I don't fucking like it.

"Okay, you need to tell me what the fuck is wrong, Emmy. I can't fix it if you don't tell me."

"You can't fix everything, Josh."

"When it comes to you, I *will* fix everything. At least let me try."

Emily turns around, crossing her arms over her chest, and my eyes are drawn to the cleavage she's practically shoving in my face.

"Argh, why the hell do you have a closet full of women's stuff?" she huffs out.

I laugh a little, trying to disguise it as a cough. "I

have women's shit in here because a woman lives here—*with me.*" I stab at my chest to signify myself.

"Who is she?" Emily stands up, looking around the closet like someone is going to pop out.

"Only the most beautiful girl I've ever laid eyes on. The smartest, bravest and most loyal person I've ever had the pleasure of meeting. Not to mention, her pussy is..."

"Stop, do not say any more unless you want to find yourself missing a beloved body part," she seethes at me.

I get up and wrap my arms around her. She tries to fight me off so I tighten my grip.

"Emmy, that girl is you, babe. The woman who lives here with me is you. The one all these clothes are for... is you."

"Me?"

"Not sure why you're having a hard time comprehending that. Yes, you."

"Where did all this stuff come from?"

"I had Ella help me out, while we were at the cabin."

"You shouldn't have done that, Josh. This must have cost you a fortune."

"In case you haven't noticed, I'm not really short on cash."

"That's not the point. If I want clothes, I can buy

them myself."

"Just a thank you would suffice, Emmy. I'm not having this argument with you. You needed shit. I got you shit. End of story."

"Really. Well, you can take it back. I don't need it."

"I'm not taking it back. It's yours. And we really need to be fucking quiet in here."

"Fine, I'll be as quiet as a damn mouse," she spits out as she sits back on the floor in front of the bench seat.

I guess we're back to braiding hair. Sitting behind her, I run the brush through her hair for a few minutes before it dawns on me that I have no fucking idea how to make a braid. I'm not going to admit that to her though. She wants her hair braided, so I'm going to figure out just how to do it. How hard can it be?

Putting the brush down, I pick up the strands of her hair and start twisting parts around each other. I'm sure I've seen girls do that. I get to the ends of her hair, and I don't know what the fuck I've done, but it doesn't look like a damn braid.

Letting the strands go, I run my fingers through her hair to separate the pieces. I slide my phone out of my pocket and pull up a YouTube tutorial on hair braiding. Emily is still quietly fuming as I watch the muted video. *Twice.*

Right, I've got this. Copying what the girl did in the video, I manage to get an end product that looks somewhat like a braid.

Emily reaches her hand around and runs her fingers down the braid. "Not bad. Not gonna lie, I didn't actually think you could braid hair. Thank you."

Well, thank fuck the silent treatment's over. "I didn't know until about five minutes ago when I watched a tutorial on YouTube."

She stands up and turns around. "You watched a tutorial, just now? To learn how to braid hair? Why?"

"Because I didn't know how to do it, and you wanted your hair braided. How else was I going to learn?"

"You really didn't need to do that. I could have done it myself."

"If you ask me to do something, Emmy, chances are I'm going to figure out how to do it."

I hear footsteps enter the bedroom. Reaching under the bench seat, I grab the Glock that I had stashed there. I shove Emily behind me and aim the gun at the door of the closet. I'm pretty sure it's going to be Sam out there, but I'm not willing to take any chances.

Seconds later, Sam opens the door. "Don't shoot." He raises his hands, laughing.

I lower the gun. "Took you bloody long enough, mate."

"I figured I'd disconnect the cameras around the place before I opened the door to the closet." Sam peers over my shoulder. "Figured you two kids would be playing seven minutes in heaven."

Emily steps out from behind me. "Oh, I played that game once in high school. It's not what it's cracked up to be."

"Back the fuck up! Who the hell played seven minutes in heaven with you?" It's not until I see the shock, the fear on her face, that I notice how loud I raised my voice.

Emily starts backing up until she hits the island in the middle of the closet. Fuck. I really need to learn to rein in my reactions. I fucking hate seeing her like this. Gone is the feisty girl who gave me hell for having women's clothes in here five minutes ago. In her place is a scared, shattered soul, afraid of what's coming next.

She shakes her head no. Her mouth opens, but no words come out. How the fuck do I fix this?

"Emmy, I'm sorry. I shouldn't have yelled." I raise my hands up, like I'm surrendering to her. Her eyes dart to the gun I'm still clutching in my right hand. Flipping it over, I hold the Glock out for her to take.

"Here, hold this for me." I'm hoping offering her a

weapon will show her I'm not about to fucking hurt her.

"Why?" she asks.

"Because, right now, you're scared. I don't like it. Take the gun, Emmy. If anyone scares you, shoot them." I grab her hand and wrap her palm around the handle of the gun.

"No, I don't want it. I don't know what's wrong with me, Josh. I can't control this. I don't know how to stop these images from running through my mind. I want it to stop. I want to stop seeing it. Make it stop, please."

I hold her face in my hands, connecting my eyes with hers. Leaning in, I kiss her forehead before pulling back. "I want to make it all better for you, Em. More than anything else in this world, I want that. But I don't know how. Tell me what I need to do to help. I'll do anything."

"You can't fix this, Josh. No one can help me. I need to figure it out for myself."

"We will figure it out together. You're not alone, Emmy."

Emily shakes her head no. "I'm sorry." She puts the gun down on the island bench behind her.

"You don't need to be sorry, babe. *I'm* sorry. I shouldn't have yelled."

"I'm not scared of you, Josh. I just forget sometimes. Some things just take me back. I don't want to be that girl anymore. I'm tired of being scared of my own shadow." Tears fall down her cheek.

"As much as I don't like seeing you scared, it's okay to be scared, Emmy. Everyone is scared of something."

"You're not scared of anything. You never have been."

"That's not true. There's one thing I'm scared of," I admit.

"What?"

"You. I'm scared I'll wake up one day and you'll be gone. I'm scared that you're going to realise just how good you really are—too good for someone like me. I'm fucking terrified of what I'll become if I lose you again."

"You've been just fine without me for the last seven years. You will survive without me again." She says it like it's already a done deal, like she already knows she's not sticking around.

"I've been anything but fine, Emmy. If I lose you again, it will ruin me."

"I don't want to ruin you, Josh."

"Then don't."

"We don't always get to say how life ends up."

"I get to say how we end up, Emmy. And in my story, we will win out over any odds."

CHAPTER 4

EMILY

"Ah, I'll leave you kids to it. I'll be in the kitchen if you need me, Emily," Sam shouts as he walks out, leaving Josh and me alone. The moment his footsteps can't be heard anymore, Josh picks me up and sits me on the island bench. Spreading my thighs apart, he places himself between them. His fingers trail their way up the outside of my legs, leaving goosebumps in their wake.

Using one hand, Josh pulls his phone out, presses a few buttons, then shows me the screen with the seven-minute timer.

"What are you doing?"

"Giving you a *seven minutes in heaven* memory to replace the other one you shouldn't have had—which, by the way, I'm gonna need a name."

"I don't know. I'm pretty fond of the first memory," I tease.

"Emmy, you do not want to poke the beast right now. Do you really think I won't go on a rampage and murder every fucking boy you went to school with?"

"That would be a lot of boys, considering I went to ten different schools. And what makes you so sure it was even with a boy?"

"Emmy, did you kiss a girl?" Josh asks, then shakes his head. "You know what... it doesn't fucking matter if it was a girl, a boy, or a fucking unicorn. Whoever it was touched something that didn't belong to them. So, name, Emmy. Who was it?"

"That name will go with me to the grave, which is exactly where you're going to be real soon if you don't shut up and kiss me already."

Wrapping my legs around his waist, I lock my ankles, one over the other, to hold him in. My arms go around his neck and drag his head towards me. My lips hungrily find his, my tongue pushing its way into his mouth. Not that he puts up any fight, his tongue eagerly swirling around my own.

My emotions are so messed up at the moment. One minute, I'm scared. The next, I'm crying. And now, I'm bloody horny as hell. I wonder if my increased libido is just a coping mechanism for escaping my own mind. Am I using Josh as an emotional outlet?

My thoughts are quickly forgotten as Josh grabs hold of my braided hair, yanking my head back and tilting my face at an angle that allows him better access. He devours me.

"Mmm." Tightening my legs, I shamelessly dry-hump him, the outline of his hard cock beneath the denim of his jeans rubbing against my clit. I can't get enough. I need more. I want more. It's always *more* with Josh. I can never be close enough.

Josh's hands reach behind him and unwrap my legs from his waist. He pulls away from my mouth, taking a step back. My body unconsciously follows his, almost causing me to fall off the damn bench.

"Why'd you stop?"

Clutching the phone, which I now notice he's holding up as it's blaring some god-awful bell alarm, he says, "Time's up, babe."

"No, I need more time, Josh. Set it again. Practice makes perfect. We should practice this whole seven minutes in heaven game." My stomach chooses this moment to make itself known, the rumble so loud it echoes in the room.

Josh laughs as he reaches out and helps me down, waiting for me to be steady on my feet. "Sorry, I need to feed you before that monster gets out."

Pain radiates through me as I put all my weight on my left foot. I wince slightly—a wince that Josh does not miss. I've been doing so well with not letting on how much my hip hurts. I can deal with the pain, block it out to a point.

"What's wrong? What happened?"

"Nothing. I'm fine. What have you got to eat in this place anyway?" I try to change the subject.

"Nice try. You're in pain. Why didn't you say something sooner? Fuck, Em. Should I get the doctor over?"

"NO! Do not go calling any more doctors. I'm fine. Trust me, I've had worse."

His face goes blank. His body stiffens. I guess that was the wrong thing to say. "Josh, I'm fine. Really. I just need to eat."

He takes a deep breath in, closes his eyes, and is he…? I think he's counting to ten in his head. When he mouths ten, he opens his eyes again. Smiling at me, he scoops me up in his arms.

"Let's get you fed."

"Put me down. I can walk."

He doesn't respond, just looks at me with his eyebrows drawn down, and shakes his head, continuing his way out to the kitchen.

Josh sits me on a bar stool at the counter, kissing my forehead before he stalks into the walk-in pantry. I swoon, like full-blown swoon. Why does being kissed on the forehead feel so good? It's such a simple gesture, yet one I haven't had in a very long time.

"What happened to you?" Sam asks me. Where did he come from? I didn't know he was even still in the apartment?

"Nothing." I smile.

"Bullshit. What happened, Emily?" he asks again, crossing his arms over his chest.

"He's being overdramatic. I fell while dismounting Cherry this morning. That's all. It's just a little bruise." I shrug my shoulders.

"There's nothing little about that bruise, Emmy. Here, take these," Josh says, holding out two white pills.

I can feel the sweat rolling down my back. They're just pills. I have to calm down. I cannot freak out again. *They're just pills,* I repeat to myself. Swallowing, my throat dry, I ask, "What are they?" My voice quakes, even though I try not to let it.

Josh screws his eyes. I can see the intake of breath

he draws before he marches over to the bin and dumps the pills. I watch as he silently walks back into the pantry, returning with a packet in his hands.

He holds the box out to me—a *sealed* box of paracetamol. "It's just paracetamol, Em. Take two."

I go to take the box, when he holds my hand still. "We will be discussing this later," he says before letting go. Sam places a glass of water down on the bench in front of me.

"Here you go, love." He winks.

Josh slaps him across the back of the head. "Her name is Emily, asshole."

"Thank you." I take two pills out of the sealed packet and swallow them. I can't look in Josh's direction right now. I know I need to trust him. And I do. But these moments I have, where I second-guess his motives, they are driving me insane. I don't know how to stop it. The guilt is drowning me. Josh has never done anything to warrant my distrust. Well, nothing to make me think he's out to hurt me… physically anyway.

He loves me. I've always known that, even when he didn't want to admit it to himself. I wonder… when did he accept the fact that he loves me? He seems to have no problem telling me now. Yet, seven years ago, he wanted me out of town.

I get that we've both grown, changed, and had

experiences that have turned us into different people. But whatever this connection is that I've always felt with Josh, it's never gone away. If anything, it's intensified now that I'm back here with him.

"So, I'm cooking. What'll it be, kids? Your options are steak, steaks, or steaaaaaaks?" Sam says, pulling a pack of steaks out of the fridge.

I laugh, appreciating that he's attempting to put a knife through the current tension both Josh and I are throwing out there. "Ahh, guess I want steak?" I question back to him.

"Right answer." He winks again.

"Emily, you can have whatever you want. Don't listen to this jerk. If you don't want steak, I'll order in. What do you want?" Josh is staring straight at me, through me, like he can see deep down to my soul. It's unnerving.

But what bothers me more than his soul-piercing gaze is the fact that he called me Emily and not Emmy. I'm not even sure why it bothers me. He's the only person who has ever called me Emmy. Everyone else will say Emily or Em. I feel like I'm going crazy. It's just a name. The fact that he called me by my name is fine. It doesn't mean anything, right?

"Don't overthink it. It's just food. There is no

right or wrong answer, Emmy. What do you want to eat?" Josh pulls me out of my own head, again.

"Steak sounds good. Although, I don't see a barbecue in this fancy apartment of yours. Can you really call it steak if you don't barbecue it?" I ask.

"Don't you worry. I got you covered. See you at the top." Sam collects a tray and walks out of the kitchen, leaving Josh and me alone.

"At the top? Where is he going?" I ask Josh.

"To the rooftop. There's a barbecue up there."

"Oh, well, should we go up with him?" I ask, hopping off the stool.

"We will," Josh says as he steps in front of me, trapping me between the bench and the brick wall of muscle that is all Josh. Reaching up, he tucks a loose strand of hair behind my ear—the gesture, soft and comforting, a total contradiction to the storm I see brewing within those ocean blue eyes of his.

"Right after you tell me about the pills." His arms fall to each side of me, before he rests his hands on the benchtop behind me. He has me trapped. I can't escape.

Looking all around, I try to find a way to flee, a way out of this. Not so much to get away from Josh, but more to get out of this conversation I do not want to be having.

"You can't run away from this, Emmy. We need

to face this head-on. And I can't fucking help you if I don't know what I'm dealing with. So, let's start with the pills."

He's right. I know he's right, yet I still can't seem to bring myself to tell him.

"You really don't want to know, Josh. It's not something I want to think about, let alone talk about. Please, just drop it. I took the paracetamol. Can't that be enough?"

"The pills, Em, why didn't you want to take the ones I tried to give you first? I saw your reaction. Fuck, I fucking felt it. The fear, mistrust, confusion that you feel, I feel it too. That shit cuts right through me. So, I need to know why. Please, let me understand why. Let me be the one to help you."

Goddamn it. "How do you do that? You make me want to tell you everything. But I'm so afraid that when I do, I'm going to wake up and find you gone. Again."

"I promise you will never wake up and find me gone. The pills, Em, why?"

I can do this; he should probably know what he's dealing with when it comes to me. I can't stay anyway, right? So, what's it matter what he thinks of me. *It doesn't.* "Okay, sometimes he would give me pills, and when I woke up, days would have passed. I lost a lot of days being unconscious." I'm looking down, not able to meet his eyes. I don't want to see the disgust reflected in them.

Josh puts his hand under my chin. "Thank you for telling me." He leans in and kisses my forehead. "I have one more question that's been eating at me."

"What?"

"Why did you marry him? Did you love him? Do you love him?" he grits out through clenched teeth.

I shake my head no. I was never in love with Trent. Lust maybe, at the start, but it was never love. "No, I didn't have a choice. I would never have married anyone if it were up to me. It wouldn't be fair to enter a marriage when your heart and soul belong to another man."

"What do you mean you didn't have a choice?"

"Two days before my twenty-second birthday. That's the first time I saw who Trent really was. He told me if I didn't sign the paper, then he would have someone pull the trigger on my mum. He... he showed me video footage of my mum in the garden —someone was watching her."

"Motherfucker!" Josh screams, taking a few steps back from me. He spins around and places his hands on the cabinet above his head. I watch his back fall and rise with each breath he takes. I knew I shouldn't have told him.

"J... Josh?" I'm not even sure what I'm asking

him. I don't know what I expect or need of him right now.

He turns around and pulls me tight into his arms. My head falls to his chest. "I'm sorry. I'm sorry. I'm sorry," I repeat over and over.

"You have nothing to be sorry for, Emmy. What happened is not your fault. I'm sorry I didn't know. I'm fucking sorry I can't torture the fucking asshole and make him feel even a tenth of the pain you've felt."

We stand there, silently clinging to each other. This is my safe place, in Josh's arms.

SITTING UP ON THE ROOFTOP, underneath the stars and twinkling fairy lights, I feel the most relaxed I have in a very long time. When Josh said there was a barbecue up here, it was the understatement of the freaking year. It's not your regular backyard barbecue area. No, it's a gourmet kitchen for the outdoors.

The back wall is lined with a stainless steel benchtop and cabinets. There's a sink and even a four-door, under-bench bar fridge. Blue LED lights frame the outline of the bench, reflecting off the stainless steel.

We're seated on a large outdoor daybed—an outdoor bed that's more comfortable than any indoor bed I've ever owned. There're strings of twinkling fairy lights hanging above that seem so out of place it makes me smile. I remember the night Josh took me back to the cabin after graduation. He had haphazardly hung fairy lights all over the place.

The way the lights are draped out here looks the same, like he has done it himself. I wonder what his fascination with fairy lights is. It's odd, yet I love them.

"Okay, kids, I'm calling it a night. Catch you tomorrow," Sam says, pulling his large frame out of the chair opposite us.

"Thank you for cooking dinner. It was delicious." I smile up at him.

"For you, I'd cook any time, Emily." He winks back at me.

"Huh." This must be what all those heroines in the reverse harem romance books feel like, having multiple men doting on them.

"*Huh,* what?" Josh asks.

"*Huh,* nothing. I just had a random thought pop into my head—nothing important." I can feel my cheeks heating up.

Josh tilts his head and squints his eyes at me, examining my every reaction. I really wish I could go back to high school me, who never let anyone see behind the walls. I need to work harder to build those walls back up.

"It was definitely something. Care to share?"

"Trust me, you really don't want to know."

"I wanna know," Sam pipes in.

"Well, I read a lot of books on my kindle, and I just thought that this must be what the heroines of reverse harem books get. Two men doing nice shit for them." I shrug my shoulders. I feel Josh's body stiffen next to me.

"No! Not a fucking chance in Hell, Emily. You know I'd do anything for you. But sharing you in some fucked-up, reverse harem shit ain't ever going to fucking happen. Fuck. I want to shoot him for just putting that thought into your head." Josh points to Sam, who is standing in front of us with his mouth hanging open.

I burst out laughing. I know that Josh is not the sharing type. Thank God for that, because I certainly do not want to be shared. "Eww, I don't want you to share me with anyone, idiot. It was a fleeting thought about the books."

"You're trying to get me killed, Emily. I knew it! You hate me. It's my cooking, isn't it? Just tell me. Be honest," Sam rambles out.

"Your cooking is fine. I mean, it's not as good as

Josh's, but it's good. And I don't hate you. I don't even know you." I take hold of Josh's hand, just in case he does have any ideas of shooting his only friend.

"Well, I'm out. Enjoy your night." I'm not sure I've seen anyone walk out of a room so fast before.

I giggle. "You should really stop threatening to shoot your friends, Josh. You won't have any left."

"I don't need any friends. I already have the best one right here." Josh stands up, pulls out his phone, presses a few buttons and "Behind Blue Eyes" by Limp Bizkit starts playing.

CHAPTER 5

JOSH

Pressing play on the music, I hold my hand out to Emily. "Dance with me." Her nose scrunches up at my request.

"You wanna dance? To Limp Bizkit?"

"Babe, I'd dance with you to any music. In fact, there doesn't even need to be music, and I'd still dance with you."

"Okay, I officially know what it means to swoon now." She takes my hand and I pull her up, out of the lounger, and to her feet.

I don't waste time before I have her little body pressed tight against me. The feel of her curves under my palms, her scent surrounding me, hearing her cute little sighs as she relaxes in my hold—this right here is my ecstasy.

I don't know how I survived living all those years without her. Actually, that's a lie. I do know. I wasn't fucking living. That became evident, really fucking fast, the minute she came crashing back into my life.

I listen to the lyrics to "Behind Blue Eyes" play softly, and the words couldn't be closer to the truth. Because I am a bad man. I don't have a conscience, but I do dream of a future. And every image I can conjure up, they all revolve around this woman.

Back in high school, I hated the feelings she evoked in me. I hated that I didn't understand them. And I fucking hated myself, knowing I couldn't do anything with them. So, I shoved them down. Loved her from the sidelines. Watched her every chance I got.

I'm not sure she even knows the extent at which I used to watch her from the shadows. But how else was I meant to protect her? To shield her from the assholes we went to school with.

Emily tips her head back and looks up at the rafters above us. "This reminds me of graduation night, all the fairy lights. Did you hang them yourself up here?"

"I did."

"Why?" she pushes. I was hoping she'd drop it. If

she didn't ask, I didn't have to admit that I've spent countless nights staring up at these lights, recalling graduation night. But she asked, and I won't ever lie to her. Omit the truth? Sometimes. If it's for her own good, sure. But lying is not something I could ever do with her.

"I like fairy lights." I shrug.

"You like fairy lights? Why?" She laughs.

"I like them because the twinkle in them reminds me of your eyes. Every time I used to get a glimpse of your blue eyes back in high school, I swore I could see a light reflecting in them. I've spent many nights up here, replaying every memory I could conjure up of your eyes."

"I don't get it. I know that you love me, Josh. I can feel your love deep down in my soul. I've never doubted it—well, maybe I've doubted it sometimes. But your love, the thought of knowing that there was still one person in the world who loved me like no other. That knowledge got me through a lot of my darkest times. But what I don't understand is why? If you love me as much as you do, then why the hell did you make me leave?"

I can feel her body stiffen the moment she finishes her question. How the hell do I answer that? That's a fucking loaded question. But when I look down into her terrified eyes, I know I have to answer her. She needs to know there isn't a damn thing she should be too afraid to ask me.

I press stop on the music and pull her into my lap as I fall back down on the lounger. My fingers run through her hair. It amazes me how it's always so soft and silky. I love the feel of it in my hands.

"I need you to promise me that whatever I say, you will hear me out until I finish. It's not a pretty story, Em, and I really would urge you to reconsider needing to hear it." I kiss her lips. I need to seal her to me. I need to feel her connection. She already has one foot out the fucking door. After hearing everything, I wouldn't be surprised if it tipped her over the edge and made her sprint for the fucking hills.

"I know that I don't say it much. But I do love you, Joshua McKinley. There is nothing you can possibly tell me that will make me think any differently of you."

Her words somewhat put me at ease. But she doesn't know what she's about to hear. I can barely think about the horrors that the McKinley dynasty was built on. How is someone as fucking perfect as she is ever going to agree to become one of us? Because whether she accepts it or not, she is mine. She is one of us. I've already instructed my team of solicitors to change my will, stating that in the event something were to happen to me, everything I own, my majority shares in McKinley Industries—it will all go to her.

"Okay. I was eighteen, Emmy. My father was still in control of everything. I had no way of protecting you. That's why I had to let you go. Because I knew if I kept you, like every fibre of my fucking being ached to, I would have been signing your death certificate. He would never have let me keep you."

It doesn't escape me that she did, in fact, have a death certificate signed anyway. Thank fuck it was a fucking forgery.

"What do you mean? What did you need to protect me from?"

"My father. The McKinley dynasty. The shady shit my father was involved in."

"What kind of shit?"

I take a deep breath. "Mostly money laundering. However, if it was underhanded, my father probably had his claws in it."

"Money laundering? Why? Your family clearly is not short on funds," she asks.

"It wasn't always about the money. It was about power. My father craved power. He controlled a lot of shady fuckers' money—who, in turn, gave him power."

"Okay, but why would you not be allowed to have a girlfriend?"

"Because love makes you weak, according to him. I had a puppy once. My mother bought it for me when I was six. She read that pets could be a way to make your antisocial child… I don't know… social? Or connect on some emotional level. Guess it's true, because it worked. I really liked that dog. The moment my father saw how much I cared for it, he made me watch as he slit the dog's throat."

"What? Holy crap, Josh, that's bloody crazy. I'm so sorry, Josh. Wait… you're not… you don't do that illegal stuff now, right?"

"I've mostly cleared the family of all of it. Em, I'm not the monster my father was. There was a time when I thought I was. I know my mother thinks we didn't know what he would do to her behind closed doors, but we could hear everything. Every slap, every kick, every word of abuse he would throw at her."

She tries to climb off me, so I hold her tighter. Her whole body tenses up. I can tell there is a question on the tip of her tongue. She's wanting to ask me something but isn't sure she should.

"Just ask me. What is it?"

"Have you ever…" She swallows, tipping her head down before continuing. "Have you ever wanted to hurt me?"

"Fuck no! All I've ever wanted to do is protect

you, Emmy. Love you. Worship you. I would rather chop off my own fucking hands than ever use them to cause you harm."

Her body relaxes slightly. "Okay. So, you work, obviously. What is it exactly that you do?"

"I'm the CEO of McKinley Industries. I'm working on cleaning up shop, as much as I can, babe. I promise nothing I do will ever affect you."

"You can't make those sorts of promises, Josh. What if you end up in jail? *What am I even saying?* I'm the one looking at spending life behind bars. I killed my husband. It doesn't even matter what you do."

Within seconds, I flip her over so she's on her back, and underneath me. I can't help the growl that leaves my mouth. "Do not say that. He was not your husband, Emily. He was a lowlife piece of shit, not worthy of breathing the same fucking air as you. And I'd put money on it that the marriage documents you signed were fake, just like your fucking death certificate."

"Do you think that's possible?" she asks hopefully.

"Yes. And even if they weren't, he was not your fucking husband."

"Okay," she agrees in a quiet voice.

I can't fucking stand the thought of her calling another man her husband. It should be me. I should be the only one she ever calls her goddamn husband. It should be my fucking last name she takes on.

"Em, when I settle all of this and shit calms down, I guarantee you will be wearing my ring. You will be using my last name. You will take the throne that's always been yours. You will be my queen."

She smiles up at me. "You know proposals are usually formatted as a question, right? Are you really going to order me to marry you? Because I've done that once—it didn't pan out too well."

Shit, Fuck. She's right. "That was not a proposal. When I ask you to marry me, Emmy, there will be no doubt that it's a question, one that I can only pray you say yes to."

I lean down and kiss her. *Claim her*. If I can't put my ring on her yet, I can claim her body as mine. And that's exactly what I need to do right now.

Pulling away from her mouth, I sit up, straddling her thighs. I run my fingertips along the middle of her breast, right down to her midsection. The yellow sundress she has on is already bunched up to the top of her thighs.

Moving backwards slightly, I pull her into a sitting position, my fingers brushing the thin straps of her dress over her shoulders.

"You know, I've always fantasised about having you up here. I've dreamt about making love to you under the stars and twinkling lights more times than I can count. Envisioned spending hours worshiping the perfection you are." I trail my tongue slowly over her collarbone and up the side of her neck.

"Mmm, yes, that. Aghh, I think you should definitely do that." Her throat vibrates as she moans.

My hands find the zipper on the back of her dress, lowering it much slower than I want to. What I want to do is tear the fucking dress in half, bend her over and fuck her until all she knows is the feel of my cock driving in and out of that sweet fucking pussy of hers.

Instead, I take my time. Emily deserves to be worshiped. And it ain't like it's a fucking hardship to worship her. Her body is the definition of a goddess. Her dress falls down past her shoulders. Pulling the straps over her arms, I let the fabric fall to her waist.

Her breasts, full D-sized breasts, call out to me, her pink nipples pebbled and just begging to have my mouth wrapped around them. Cupping my palms over each breast, I feel the weight of them in my hands. I roll my fingers across the globes, without touching her hardened nubs.

The moment her back arches, offering those rosy buds to me on a fucking platter, I don't hold back. Leaning down, I take her right nipple into my mouth, twirling my tongue around it while gently biting down. My fingers pinch and pull on her left nipple, the sounds coming out of her mouth filling the otherwise quiet night air.

"Mmm, I could spend all night just licking and sucking on these breasts." I bite down a little harder before I move my mouth to the other side. Emmy moans, her thighs tightening underneath mine.

I'm still hovering above her legs, mindful not to make contact with the bruising on her hip. But she can't move them and it's driving her insane. Smiling around her nipple, I can't help but chuckle at how much she's trying to get friction between her thighs.

"Josh, I need..."

Releasing her nipple with an audible pop, I ask her, "What do you need, Emmy?" I want her to ask for it. I want her to fucking beg me for it. My tongue goes back to lapping at her nipple, licking all around the hardened tip.

"Mmm, you know what I need."

"I'm not a mind reader, Em. You're gonna have to say it if you want it."

"Argh, Josh, I need you to touch me." She groans as I bite down slightly on her nipple.

"I am touching you." I massage her breast with both hands.

"Damn it, Josh! I need you to touch my pussy, okay? I need you to make me come!" she screams.

I smile. This is what I wanted. Her so far out of her mind with chasing that pleasure that she's not afraid to say what she wants, to ask for what she needs. "Say *please*." I smirk at her.

Her eyes tighten and her jaw tenses as she spits out, "*Please*."

Laughing, I move my leg, placing it between her thighs to hold them open.

Lowering my hand, I slip my fingers underneath the lace of her panties. Her pussy's already dripping wet, soaking my fingers instantly. My mouth never leaves her nipple, sucking, licking and biting down. Inserting two fingers into her channel, I flatten my palm on her clit and hold still.

I bring my mouth up to her neck, and nibbling on her ear, I whisper, "I want you to ride my hand, Emmy. I want your juices dripping down my wrist. Make yourself come on my fingers, Em. Take what you need from me, before I bury my cock so far into your pussy and take everything from you."

"Mmm, J-Josh." She lets out a mixture of groans and moans as her hips start rotating, her pussy tightening, clenching around my fingers and drawing them in and out. She grinds her clit harder into my palm.

I move my lips back down to her breast, using my free hand to squeeze and pinch one nipple while my mouth devours the other. Her moans get louder, her movements more frenzied. She's close. I bite down harder on one nipple while twisting the other. She detonates, her juices dripping down my fingers. I hold my hand still, until I feel her relax.

Her head's thrown back, her mouth open in that beautiful O-shape. This is a look I want to see on her face every fucking day for the rest of my life. This look right here… she's free. At peace, no demons haunting her, no internal war happening, no struggling with what she wants versus what she thinks she should do.

I watch as her whole body relaxes as I lay her back. Her head rests on a pillow, her blonde hair falling like a golden fucking halo around her. I always knew Emmy was too good for me; she's way too fucking pure to be around someone like me. But I don't give a fuck about any of that. She is mine. And mine, she will be staying.

Pulling my fingers out of her, I bring them to my mouth. The taste of her on my tongue, I've never tasted anything as delicious as Emmy. I can't get enough of her, no matter how much I have.

I loosen the zipper on my jeans and free my raging fucking cock from its confines. I pull on the lace that's covering her pussy, tearing it in half. Lining myself up with her entrance, I look towards her face and wait. She's out of it, that orgasm disorienting her momentarily. There's no fucking way I'm entering her without her knowledge. I really fucking hope it doesn't take too long for her to come back to me, because this is testing my restraint like nothing else ever fucking has.

CHAPTER 6

EMILY

I come to with a grin on my face, my body feeling relaxed. The first thing I see when I open my eyes is Josh's smiling, if not strained, face looking down at me.

"Welcome back, Em."

"Ah, thanks?" I have no idea what I'm meant to say. But waking up with Josh hovering above me, this is something I could get used to. Wrapping my arms around his neck, I pull his mouth down to mine. He doesn't exactly put up any resistance. His tongue invades my mouth, and the taste of me on him is overwhelming, arousing. I never thought I'd like my own taste, but tasting it on Josh's tongue is on another level.

"Mmm." The moan slips from me. My hips move underneath him. I can feel his thick head waiting at my entrance. What's he waiting for? Why is he holding back? Tilting my hips, I wrap my legs around his waist, pulling him into me.

His cock stretches the walls of my pussy, the slight sting settling as soon as he's buried all the way in. Josh lifts his head, pulling away from my mouth.

"Fuck, Em, your pussy is the best thing in the fucking world. So warm and wet. The perfect place for my cock to be, really. He should live here forever."

I laugh as Josh leans back in and claims my mouth. No, he doesn't just claim my mouth. He claims all of me. My heart, my soul. He doesn't know that every fibre of my being has always been and always will belong to him and only him. Even when I tried dating other men, it was always him my heart belonged to.

Josh starts to pump in and out of me slowly, ever so slowly. It feels amazing. I can feel his love through his soft, deliberate movements. His frenzied kiss slows, and everything else slows down with it. It's just him and me. Nothing else matters in this moment. It consumes me, this love I have for him, and if I let it, it will take over. I'll go back to being the woman who blindly follows a man. I can't let myself become her again.

Shaking the gloomy thoughts from my mind, I pull myself back into the moment. I let my hands travel up and under Josh's shirt, the feel of his hard abs beneath my palms. Snaking my hands around his back, I hug him closer to me. I want him closer. Always.

I let myself enjoy this moment. My eyes focus on the fairy lights above and I'm taken back to the first time we made love like this. Even if I had known I'd wake up alone, I still would have spent the night with him. If I'm honest with myself, I would have followed him anywhere that night. I still would...

LYING HERE in Josh's arms, my head resting on his chest while looking up at the stars, I feel peace like I haven't for a very long time. I also feel dread. This sensation is too good to be true. I know it's going to come crashing down around my feet soon. I just don't know when.

My eyes are getting droopy, but I'm too afraid to let myself fall asleep.

"Josh?"

"Yeah, babe?" He leans down and kisses my forehead. Damn it, why does this little gesture make me want to cry? Happy tears, tears of relief.

"You're going to be here when I wake up, right?" I know I sound like a desperate, whiney, stage-five clinger. But I need to know. I'm going out of my freaking mind.

Josh puts his fingers under my chin, tilting my head up until my watery eyes meet his concerned ones. "There is nowhere else I'm going to be. I promise, Emmy, when you wake up, I'll be right here. Holding you. Probably watching you sleep like the creeper I am." He smirks before leaning down and gently kissing my lips.

"Thank you." I settle my head back on his chest and let my eyes fall closed.

"No need to thank me, babe. It's not exactly a hardship holding you in my arms. I love you, Em."

"I know," I reply.

"I know too," Josh says back. It should be easier for me to tell him I love him. I've said the words before; he must know that I do. Yet, something holds me back from uttering the phrase.

"EMMY, get up. Come on. Put this on." I'm jolted awake to Josh's panicked voice. He's standing above me, holding out my dress he discarded last night.

"What's wrong?" I ask, taking the dress and doing my best not to let panic overtake me. Jesus, if Josh looks this panicked... whatever it is, it must be bad.

"Come on, follow me. Do not let go of my hand, unless I tell you to run. If I tell you to run, you fucking run, Emmy." And I'm officially freaked the hell out. I take his hand, silently following him.

The sun has barely risen, and fog fills the rooftop. Josh swipes up his wallet and both of our phones from the bench. Turning, he tucks my phone down the front of my dress, resting it between my cleavage.

"If anything happens, call Sam or Dean. I've programmed both numbers into your contacts." He turns and starts pulling me towards the opposite side of the rooftop. The door he's leading us to is not the one we came through last night.

"Josh, you're scaring me. What's happening?" My voice trembles. I try my best not to let my fear overtake me. I can't be the helpless, defenceless woman anymore. I won't let myself be her. I need to take control.

He stops, turning and placing his palms against each side of my face. He leans in and kisses my lips.

"I'm sorry. I'm not trying to scare you, Em, and I promise I'll tell you everything that's happening... just as soon as I get you out of here. We don't have time to waste, come on."

Okay, here's to that whole blindly following Josh anywhere theory. Because that's exactly what I do. I don't question him any further. I simply grip his hand, like it's the only thing keeping me grounded, and let him lead me to God only knows where.

He cracks open a heavy steel door, peeking inside before pulling me in behind him. Holding his finger up to his lips, he gestures for me to be quiet. We then make our way down flight after flight of stairs. By around the tenth flight, I'm having a hard time keeping up with him. My hip is aching so badly I just want to crumble to the floor.

I can't though. I have to push through the pain, through the exhaustion. Josh notices I'm having difficulties. He turns around and mouths, "Hold on," to me before bending at the waist and throwing me over his shoulder, carrying me down the stairs at a much quicker pace than what we were going.

The speed he is managing to run down these stairs while carrying me is impressive, to say the least. How has he not collapsed yet? Stopped to catch his breath? God, I feel pathetic... I couldn't even keep up with *walking* down all these levels.

We get to the bottom and he settles me on my feet, before opening the door and peeking through it again. Once he deems it okay, he leads me into a garage. A nice bloody garage, with two rows of very expensive sports cars. Josh stops at a sleek, black, Batmobile-looking car. When he presses a button and the doors open upward, I'm almost certain it *is* the damn Batmobile.

He supports me as I lower myself into the car. I can't help but look into every shadow in this place, waiting for something or someone to jump out. When Josh jogs around the front of the car, climbing into the driver's seat, I finally let out the air I was holding in my lungs. It's going to be okay.

I stay silent as Josh starts the ignition, the engine roaring so loudly I can barely hear my own thoughts. *So much for being quiet.* I look over at his profile. His jaw is tense, his eyes scanning every direction as he manoeuvres the car out of the underground garage.

As soon as he hits the street, he floors it. My whole body gets pulled back into the seat, the engine's vibrations coming through the leather interior. He makes a few quick turns before slowing down a little. He's still tense. I don't know what I can do to help. I should be able to help... Whatever it is that's happening, it's because of me.

I reach over and place my hand on top of his. He shifts down gears and brings the car to what would be an acceptable speed. He lifts my hand, raising my fingers to his mouth, and kisses lightly.

"Josh, did you steal the Batmobile? Because I'm pretty sure Batman is not someone *even you* want to mess with," I ask.

Josh's laugh fills the car and his body relaxes more as he settles back into his seat. "No, this car is way better than the Batmobile, babe. This beauty right here is a Lamborghini Aventador, so much better than the Batmobile." He shakes his head, as if the thought of me not knowing what type of car we are in is inconceivable.

"Um, Josh? What happened back there?" I ask tentatively.

"Uh, there were some uninvited guests in the penthouse. I'm sorry I scared you, Em. But you are safe. I promise I will not let anyone hurt you ever again."

"Are you safe though? Is me being here going to end up hurting you? I can't do that to you, Josh. It's not fair."

He turns his head so fast to face me. "The only thing that can ever hurt me, Em, is you leaving. Not being able to wake up next to you every day, that's what will hurt me. No, it won't just hurt me. It will fucking ruin me. Don't do it."

He's pleading for me not to leave. I know that if I did, it would destroy him. But then again, I might just end up destroying him if I stay. "I don't want to leave. I want to wake up next to you every day. I'm going to fight this. I'm going to figure out a way to get myself out of this mess."

"*We*, babe. We are going to figure this out."

"Where are we going now?" I ask. It looks like we're heading into the suburbs, only not the normal, everyday people suburbs. This is the elite, rich people with mansions for guest houses kind of suburbs.

"Somewhere no one will be able to find us. But ah, how good are you at climbing fences? You're good with heights, right?"

"Fences? Heights? Uh, I can climb a fence. You know I was part of the gymnastics club at school. I think I'll survive the heights. Why? Whose fence are we scaling?"

"Emmy, you were in every fucking club at school. We're breaking into the McKinley Residence."

"Ah, Josh, have you forgotten that you are a McKinley? Why do we need to sneak in?"

"So no one knows we're there, of course." He winks at me.

"Don't Dean and Ella live in that house?" I'm sure Ella told me about some museum-type house Dean had her move into.

"Yes, which is why we are sneaking inside. It'll be okay." He pulls the car up to the side of the road. Looking into the rear-view mirror, he says, "Okay, let's do this. Wait until I open your door." With that, he jumps out and runs around the front of the car.

Once I'm out of the car, I notice we are not alone. Sam is leaning against a black SUV, smiling a huge-ass smile.

"Rules: Do not go over fifty kilometres an hour. Stop at every fucking orange light. If you so much as leave a hair in it, you buy it. Got me?" Josh grunts out. Huh, I guess he's protective over his car.

"Sure thing, boss. Although, you and I both know you don't pay me enough to buy one of these beauties. Emily, lovely to see you as always." Sam smirks in my direction.

"Ah, you too?" My response comes out as more of a question than a statement.

"Come on, I'm going to show you how to break and enter into one of the most-guarded, high-tech security homes in this neighbourhood." Josh grabs my hand and leads me up the street.

We stop at a tall green hedge. Josh runs his hands along the hedge until his arm disappears between the manicured leaves. "This way." He tilts his head, pushing his way through the bush. He stands on the other side, holding both arms out to make a walkway for me.

"Wow, Moses parted the seas. Joshua McKinley parted the hedge. I always thought you were god-like." I laugh.

"You know very well I'm not just god-like, Emmy. I am a fucking god." He laughs. Taking hold of my hand, he starts jogging across a large green lawn. And I mean large. It's more like a footy oval than a back yard. I stumble as I try to keep up. Josh slows down.

"Don't even think about it. I can walk," I growl at him just as he was about to pick me up again.

"Yes, boss." He holds his hands up in a surrender motion, before looking at his watch. "We have exactly three minutes until the guards make their way to this side of the yard. Come on."

"Guards?" Shit, that does not sound like a good thing. I follow Josh, jogging across the yard. When we finally stop at the wall of a building, I'm heaving with sweat dripping down my forehead. Did we just run ten kilometres? Shit, I'm out of shape. When I look up at Josh, who hasn't even broken a sweat nor seems remotely winded, I get mad. Like irrationally pissed off.

"I hate you. You know that. Did we really need to run across the yard? Some people are allergic to exercise, just so you know. For future reference, I'm one of those people."

"You're extremely hot when you're angry. I just got a level-ten boner from that little tirade." He smirks, adjusting himself in his pants.

"What the hell is a level-ten? Are there actually different levels? No, wait... don't answer that."

"Okay, when we go through this door, stick as close to the wall as possible. Don't make a sound. The cameras will pick up any sound. The way we are going, they won't be able to see us, but if we talk, you bet they'll record that."

My face must look as terrified as I feel, because Josh leans down and kisses me. The moment his lips meet mine, I can feel my anxiety start to ease, slightly. "It's okay, Em. I own this house, remember? We're not actually breaking in, more like *sneaking in,* so mum and dad won't hear us."

"Okay, but this is Dean and Ella's home, right? It still feels wrong to be sneaking in."

"It's a family property. Dean and Ella just happen to live in this one. Besides, it's not like Ella is going to kick her favourite brother-in-law out on the streets." He smiles, so sure of himself.

CHAPTER 7

JOSH

Emmy's grip on my hand is tight. I'm afraid she's going to cut off the circulation in my damn fingers. It's admirable how she feels like she's doing something wrong. Maybe to some people it would seem wrong to sneak into the house your brother lives in. I just don't give a fuck. The way the McKinley trust works is everyone has their shares. I inherited the majority shares, so in actuality, I own the *majority* of this house.

Besides, I'm not afraid of getting caught. I have a secret weapon up my sleeve when it comes to handling my brother now. She comes in the form of a brunette spitfire, who can literally kick my ass.

Ella. Yep, my brother's new bride happens to be very fond of me. She'd never boot me out of here, or let Dean try to either.

I could have walked through the front door, but what would be the fun in that? Besides, I want Emmy to myself for a bit. I need time to process what the fuck I'm going to do about this fucking cop who seems to be able to get into my penthouse. A penthouse in a building that is meant to have state-of-the-fucking-art biometric security measures in place. Not to mention, the fucking armed guards who are on my payroll. How the fuck is this fucker getting past all of that?

I squeeze Emily's hand a little, attempting to reassure her that she is okay. That *we* are okay. We will be okay. I will find a way to fix this. Walking down the hallway, I go left, heading to the east wing of the house. A wing that no one ever goes into, apart from me. This has always been my sanctuary when we had to stay in this house, as well as during the countless times I've stumbled in here drunk off my ass, making Dean handle my shit for me when I was too fucking wasted to do anything.

There were a few years after I made Emily leave town where I was wrecked. I drank every night, took whatever drug I could get my hands on, anything that would make me forget. And when you're an eighteen-year-old billionaire, there is no such thing as a drug you can't get your hands on.

For around a year and a half, I drank until I could forget. The only problem? It never fucking worked. No matter how much I drank, what drug I took, every time I closed my eyes, I could see her. She was in every shadow of every corner. Some nights, I'd sneak into the school and sit at the table where we first met. I'd wait like she'd walk through the doors again and we could have a second chance. I could redo everything and just claim her from that first moment.

I probably wouldn't have snapped out of it, had Dean not locked me in a fucking cell for a whole damn month. Yes, literally locked me in the fucking basement to dry me out. He kept me fed, clothed. I had all the luxuries I could want for. Just not the alcohol or drugs I used as a bandage. It worked. By the time he let me out, I had come to terms with my fuck up.

I would live the rest of my life regretting my decision to run her out of town. But I have her back now, and I will slaughter anything I conceive as a fucking threat. Finally getting to the door of my room here, I push it open (expecting the room to be empty), only to find my fucking brother sitting on the edge of the bed, waiting with a fucking grin I'd like to slap off his face.

"You're losing your touch. I knew before you even made it to the building." He laughs.

"Yeah, well, I had to adjust my route and pace. Can we not do this now? I've got shit I need to do." Pulling Emily into the room, I cling to her hand, afraid if I let go, she'll run the other way. I know my brother scares her. I don't fucking understand why, but he does, so I hold her hand tighter.

"I'm sure you do." Dean looks at Emily and then pulls his phone out of his pocket.

"El, can you come up to Josh's room?" We only hear one side of the conversation, but after a few back and forwards, he hangs up—right before the door bursts open.

"Josh, you're here?" Ella comes up and hugs me before slapping me on the chest, to which, I swear I hear Emily growl. I pull her tight against me, wrapping my arm around her shoulder.

"Ella, why don't you take Emily to the kitchen and get her a drink," Dean says.

Ella spins around, hands on her hips. Whatever she was about to say falls dead on her lips as Dean adds a "please" to his demand.

"Well, since you said please and all, but just so you know, I'm not doing this because you told me to.

I'd much rather hang out with her than you two anyway." Ella stomps her foot as she spins back around and tugs on Emily's arm. "Come on, let's get some coffee. Have you eaten breakfast yet?"

Emily looks back to me for guidance on what she should do. I hate seeing her so insecure and indecisive. I give her a slight nod. "I'll meet you down in the kitchen in a few. Save me some bacon."

"Okay." Emily gives a small smile back.

"I wasn't offering to cook for you, Josh," Ella adds as they both walk out the door.

I turn back to face Dean. Leaning against the wall, I fold my arms over my chest and wait. I'll stand here and wait him out. Whatever he's got to say, I'm sure it's going to piss me off, which is why he had Ella take Emily out of the room.

Dean attempts to stare me down for a few minutes, silently, before he gives in and shakes his head. "Do you want to explain why I had a cop at the club looking for Emily?" he asks.

My back goes ramrod stiff. Did this fucker tell them she was with me? I'll fucking kill him, brother or not. If he's put Emily at any kind of risk, I'll enjoy choking the life out of his fat neck.

"Relax. Put your fucking murderous thoughts away. I didn't tell them anything. I would like to know why we're apparently hiding out a fugitive though." He raises his eyebrow at me.

"She's not a fucking fugitive. And don't worry about it. I'll fix it. It doesn't concern you."

"It doesn't concern me?" Dean stands and starts pacing the room. "That's where you're wrong. It concerns you, which means it very much concerns me. What exactly are you planning on doing, Josh? I'd like a heads up if my little brother's planning a killing spree, targeting every detective out looking for his girl."

"I'm not going to kill every detective in the country, idiot. I don't have that sort of time. Besides, there's only one looking for her." I shrug. One who I very much intend on feeding to my damn pigs. Would that make my pigs cannibals? Because they'd be eating a pig?

"Why does she have *one* detective looking for her. What'd she do?" he asks.

I consider not telling him. This isn't really my secret to tell after all. But for some reason, I spill the beans. "She killed her husband." I shrug, with a huge grin on my face. I'm fucking damn proud of Emily for doing what she did. That takes guts. It's one thing to have thoughts of killing someone, but to actually go through with it is a whole other level.

"The fact that you're grinning about that is fucking weird, even for you."

"He was an abusive fuck who used her as a punching bag, among other things I don't care to repeat. I won't let her go down for this. I'll do whatever I have to do to get her out of this mess."

"That's what worries me." Dean stops his pacing, standing right in front of me. "I know more than anyone that there is nothing you wouldn't do for that girl. But that knowledge scares the shit out of me. I don't like worrying about you, Josh. Promise me you won't do anything stupid. Well, more stupid than usual."

"You know I can't promise that."

"Well, let me help. Who is this detective after her?" he asks. His eyes scrunch before adding, "Wait… if she killed her husband, why isn't there a nationwide manhunt for her? There wouldn't be just one cop looking for her."

"You don't think I've thought of that? The fucker was a cop, Dean. There's no way her face wouldn't be plastered on every news channel if they were looking for her. No, this detective wants something else. I just need to figure out what."

"Her husband was a cop? Someone's gotta be covering this shit up, but why?"

I shrug. *Fuck if I know*. "Either he's not dead, and

she didn't actually kill him, which I hope is the case because I'd love to get my hands on the bastard. Or there's a chance it's got something to do with Emily's trust that disappeared without a goddamn trace three years ago."

"What trust?" Dean knows she didn't come from money.

"The five million dollar trust I set up in her name. Someone withdrew it from her account the day she turned twenty-two. The day after a fake death certificate was lodged."

"So, Emily Livingston is legally dead? Then why the fuck is a cop looking for a dead girl?"

"Because it was that same cop who identified the body for the death certificate. He doesn't want Emily; he wants something from her. And I'm going to figure out what it is, exactly."

"*We* will figure it out. You're not going off alone on this, Joshua. I want to be kept in the loop on all your plans. Come on, let's head downstairs before Ella burns our kitchen down."

"I'll meet you there. I gotta make a call."

"Don't do anything stupid."

"I never do." I smirk.

I wait for Dean to leave the room before I pull my phone out and dial Sam. He picks up on the second ring.

"I'm gonna need a pay raise, boss, or a Christmas bonus in the form of this car," he yells over the sound of the engine.

"I swear to God I will fucking shoot you if you hurt my car, Sam. Now tell me you have something for me," I grunt out.

"I thought you'd never ask. But since you asked so nicely, I'll share what I've found. I'll remind you I missed sleep last night for this."

"Sam, get to it."

"Okay, don't get your knickers in a twist. So, I was able to trace the IP address. The cameras were feeding to a docking warehouse in Botany. The fucker's been getting in and out of the apartment by the fire escape door. He's managed to rewire the passcode. I've since fixed it; he won't be getting back in through that door. CCTV caught a glimpse of him entering the building. It's that lovely detective friend of yours."

"We won't be coming back to the apartment. I won't put Emily at risk like that. Text me the address of the docking warehouse."

"Will do, but it's going to be like finding a needle in a haystack there, mate. It's a shipping container dock. I was able to trace the IP back to that particular dock, but finding where it is within that warehouse is anyone's guess."

"I don't care if I have to burn that whole fucking place down to draw the fucker out. Get me the address."

"Okay, will do."

"And, Sam?" I wait for him to answer.

"Yeah?"

"I mean it about my fucking car, not a fucking scratch." Hanging up the phone, I head for the kitchen to find Emily.

CHAPTER 8

EMILY

Ella makes one hell of a cup of coffee, although I'm not sure how much of that is her actual skill set, and how much is that fancy as hell machine she used. Either way, I inhale the warm liquid gold my life depends on.

What Ella doesn't do too well is cook bacon. The whole kitchen is currently filled with smoke as we both frantically wave towels around, trying to… Actually, I don't know what we're trying to do, but it seemed like the right thing to do after I turned off the stove and threw the frying pan into the sink.

We probably look stupid, both of us laughing as we try to ease the smoke. That is, until I notice Dean standing in the entryway watching us. As soon as I see him standing there, the panic sets in. Oh shit, what have I done? Five minutes in his house and the kitchen is nearly burnt down.

I know I wasn't the one cooking, but I still feel responsible. My legs take steps backwards, as if on their own accord. I just need to put space between us. More space, I need more space. I walk backwards until I hit a counter. My eyes never leave Dean. Although I know it's Dean, the face I'm staring at now is not his.

It's Trent. He's here and I've messed up. I can see his smirk, the twitch in his eye. That same one he gets right before he lashes out at me. I've just given him a reason to get mad. I should know better. I shake my head. I try to open my mouth, try to apologise, but nothing comes out. I can't form the words.

I can see him getting closer. He's closing the distance. He's getting too close. I desperately look around for a way out. A way to get more distance. Maybe if I can find somewhere to hide until he's calmed down… except I'm trapped. I've backed myself up into the corner of the room.

I sink to my knees before he reaches me. I see a hand come out towards my face and I scream. I scream so loud. Hopefully (this time) the neighbours will hear. Someone will hear and help me. Someone has to help me. The hand never makes contact. Something's wrong. Something's different. Why hasn't he hit me yet?

I bring my knees up to my chest and sink my face into my thighs. Closing my eyes, I wait for the abuse to start. It's bound to start soon. I don't understand why he's taunting me.

"What the fuck did you do?" A loud voice roars—a loud voice that shouldn't be here. Josh, he's not supposed to be here.

"Emmy. Emmy, baby, look at me. You are okay. You are safe." Josh's voice is soft. I can feel his hands on me. Maybe I'm dreaming. Maybe Trent knocked me out and I'm dreaming. That's the only explanation I can think of right now. Except, when those hands gently lift my chin, forcing my face up, my eyes connect with those stormy blue eyes—the eyes that hold the other half of my soul.

"Josh?" How did he find me? I look around. I'm not in my apartment. This kitchen is way too fancy to be anything I've ever lived in. Then it all comes back to me: the coffee, the bacon, the smoke, Dean.

I can see Dean and Ella both staring down at me with expressions that look like pity. I don't want or deserve their pity. I look back into Josh's eyes.

"It's me, babe. You are safe," he says, kissing my forehead.

"Josh, can we go back to your room?" I need to get out of here. I need to get away from everyone else. I know I'm putting a lot on Josh right now. I shouldn't be using him as my crutch, but that's exactly what he's become. My lifeline, my sanity. He seems to be able to break me out of any panic attack I've had. When I wake up in the middle of the night from the nightmares, he's the one there, holding me and letting me cry myself back to sleep in his arms.

"Sure thing. Hold on." I feel his arms scoop me up. I bury my head in his chest. I can't bear to look at Ella or Dean right now.

"I'll bring some food up. Don't worry, I won't cook it," Ella says as we pass them.

"Thanks," Josh replies, walking out of the room with me in his arms, again.

It's been two weeks since my little breakdown in the kitchen. I haven't stepped foot out of this room. I mean, it's like there's no need to leave this room. It's bigger than the apartment I had back in Adelaide.

There's a large four-poster bed in the middle of the room, and dark wooden beams with white curtains falling down the sides of the bed. Above the bed are fairy lights, strung from beam to beam. It's a lot more feminine than I ever thought Josh would have. But it's like a fairy tale, romantic even. I love it.

The room has its own sitting area with black, plush, leather couches facing a large television that's mounted to the wall. There's even a little kitchenette-bar area off to one corner. It's fully stocked with every beverage you could probably dream of. I haven't touched a drop of alcohol though. I'm not really sure why, but the thought of it makes me want to puke, ever since the last time I tried to drink with Ella and her sisters.

It's late. I'm looking out the window, waiting for Josh to come home. I haven't told him of my growing anxiety every time he leaves. I don't ask him to stay with me, even though I desperately want him to. I know he tells me he's going into the office to do some work, and I do think that at some point during the day he does. But that's not all he's doing.

I know he's out looking for this Detective Jones. I've heard the phone calls he's been having with Sam. I know Josh is frustrated he can't find him. I've been racking my brain for any recollection of someone named Jones. I can't for the life of me make a connection between that detective and Trent.

Josh says it's awfully suspicious that there is no warrant out for my arrest—he had Sam hack into the police database to check. There is nothing on the database to report Trent's death at all. His records show that he is MIA, missing in action. I have this awful fear that I didn't actually kill him and he's out there somewhere, looking for me.

I asked Josh to look into Trent's brother. He was also a cop. According to Sam's research, he's still going about his everyday life. He goes to work and returns home to his family, which, by the way, I had no idea even existed. I met the guy heaps in the first year of dating Trent, and never once did either of them mention any other family members. Sam says that Trent's brother has a wife and two young kids.

Why hasn't he been looking for Trent? Why hasn't he alerted anyone that he's missing or anything? And, my biggest question, where is the fucking body? Josh had a team enter the apartment I shared with Trent. They found nothing; the apartment was completely empty. No furniture, no clothes, nothing. No body rotting on the kitchen floor. Just nothing. The apartment had been cleaned out.

I know he's stressed out. And I know the cause of that stress is me. I've offered to help him. If this detective is after me, why not just call and tell him a place where I'll be. I'll meet with him, see what he wants. Josh, of course, won't even consider using me for bait.

It's 11:00 p.m. now. He's been gone for fourteen hours. Fourteen long hours, in which I have to try to pretend that I'm okay without him. I have taken about six baths today, in an attempt to calm my thoughts. What if something has happened to him? I could text him. Sometimes, when it gets too much, I text him and he calls me straight away, his voice soothing my inner demons.

I don't though. I don't want to be the needy girlfriend. Is that what I am to Josh, his girlfriend? I know he's used the term before, but we've never discussed a label for what we are, other than Josh claiming that I am now and always have been *his*.

I had Ella show me how to use Facebook on this phone today. I missed out on all the social media blasts from the last few years. She introduced me to TikTok a few days ago. I'm afraid to admit how many hours I've wasted on that app. It just draws you in and keeps you there.

Today I made a fake profile on Facebook. I friended a heap of randoms who live in Adelaide. I also friended Trent's brother (Stephen) and his wife (Veronica). I searched through both profiles. Nothing on their pages mentions Trent. It's like he didn't even exist. I can't find a trace of him online anywhere.

I sent a friend request off to Detective Jones. He

hasn't accepted it yet, but I want to try to help figure out what he wants with me. Maybe then Josh can stop looking. He can stop being stressed out.

The rattle of the door handle has my heart beating overtime, until I see Josh walk in and I'm immediately overcome with relief. There's always this niggling feeling that he's just not going to come back one day. I can't seem to shake the thought.

I run up to him and jump into his arms, wrapping my own around his neck and my legs around his waist. I cling to him. Burying my face in the crook of his neck, I inhale his scent. He's freshly showered. He smells like sandalwood, the fancy shower gel he uses all the time. There have been many days he comes home in different clothing than he left in, always freshly showered.

He left wearing a suit. He's returned wearing a pair of black denim jeans and a white t-shirt. Inhaling the intoxicating scent, I ask, "Did you just shower?" before lifting my head to look him eye to eye.

He nods. "I did."

"Why?"

He thinks about it for a moment, then he answers, "Because I like to wash the filth of my world off before I come home to you."

"What'd you do today?"

"I went to the office, you know, ran a multibillion-dollar corporation. Made the McKinley family more money. The usual." He walks over to the bed, laying me down and falling on top of me.

He starts kissing me up the side of my neck. His attempts at distracting my thoughts always bloody work. As his teeth graze the sensitive skin just under my ear, my whole body shivers with pleasure. My back arches up. Pushing my pelvis into his crotch, I can feel his hardness in his jeans.

The denim rubs against my bare pussy. I purposely didn't wear panties under my dress today. Josh tends to end up tearing them anyway. One of his hands trails up my thigh until it reaches my wet centre.

Josh's body freezes above me. He groans. "Em, please tell me you haven't been walking around the house without panties on all day. Fuck, I'm going to have to shoot anyone who looked at you today," he grunts as his fingers enter me.

"Mm, no one saw me. I didn't leave the room. Well, Ella came in here for a bit. But other than that, no one saw me today. Mm, God, that... Don't stop... that," I moan as he works his fingers in and out of me.

Oh God, I'm going to come embarrassingly soon at this rate. I don't know what it is with Josh, but I can't seem to get enough of him. He's turned me insatiable. It's his own fault, really. If he wasn't so damn good at what he does, then I wouldn't want it as much.

"I'm never going to stop, Emmy. I want you to drip all over my fingers. I want to lick your juices off them. Savour the taste of you in my mouth. In fact…" Josh removes his fingers. I start to protest until I see his head move south.

Yes, *this,* I can get behind. He doesn't waste time before his tongue is circling my clit. He slides two fingers into me while sucking and nibbling on my clit. I'm so close. I'm chasing the edge of the cliff as I shamelessly push my pelvis harder into his face, my centre clenching down on his fingers as I detonate around him.

"Oh my God, Josh, yes, yes, yes!" I scream as my vision blurs. My whole body quakes with my orgasm.

Josh continues to lick until I'm nothing but a spun-out ragdoll, sprawled across the bed. When I open my eyes, Josh is hovering above me, waiting. He always waits. He never enters me until I either take over and make the decision for him, or I nod, giving him the go-ahead. I appreciate him even more for always waiting for me to be well aware of what's happening.

But I don't want him there right now. No, I want him inside my mouth first. I'm starving for a taste of him. I push him onto his back and climb down his body. Holding his shaft in one hand, I slowly stroke him up and down.

My tongue licks the precum spilling off his tip. "Mmm." God, I love the taste of him. I never thought I'd ever like the taste of a man, but Josh is different. I can't get enough of him. Not having the patience to tease him tonight, I open my mouth wide over the thick, hard head of his cock, flattening my tongue as I suck his length in as far as I can take him. I wrap my hand around the base, squeezing and stroking up and down to match the movements of my mouth.

I hollow out my cheeks and moan as his head hits the back of my throat. Attempting to relax my gag reflex to take him even further, I manage to swallow around him.

"Fuck me. Jesus, goddamn, Em," Josh grunts out as his hands reach down, picking me up from underneath my arms. My mouth leaves his cock. I can't help the pout that I'm now sporting. He smirks at me. "Babe, I was about to come down your throat."

Josh rolls us so I'm beneath him, positioning his cock at my entrance. "I need to be buried deep inside you. Are you ready for me, Emmy?"

"More than ready. Do your best, Josh, please."

CHAPTER 9

JOSH

"Do your best, Josh, please." As soon as the words leave her lips, I slam into her. The warm, wet, tight sensations making my balls constrict. I hold steady, buried to the hilt, calming my raging cock down a bit. I refuse to lose control this early. I'm not a fucking rookie teenager.

Once I've got things calmed down a little, I start pumping in and out of her, her juices dripping as the sound of flesh hitting flesh rings out loud in my ears. I needed this tonight more than she will ever know. The knowledge that I could come home and lose myself in this girl is what has kept me going these last couple of weeks.

I clear my thoughts of anything that isn't her, isn't us. This thing between Emily and me is lethal. It has the potential to ruin me. This one woman can bring me to my knees, shatter my already black soul. God help the world if it ever comes to that. Yet the rewards of having her far outweigh the risk.

"Oh God, yes, that. Keep doing that," Emily moans as she pulls on my neck, claiming my mouth. Her kiss is hungry, needy. I push my tongue deep into her mouth, giving her everything. Every piece of me belongs to her.

Our bodies move in sync, her hips arching off the bed. Pulling away from her, I sit up, lifting her legs and holding them in the air, her ankles resting on my shoulders. I hammer into her. I give her what she wanted.

Her head falls back, her eyes close and her mouth opens as I continue to pump in and out. We're both a sweaty mess, both panting for breath, climbing that hill and pursuing that ecstasy we can only get as we crash over the cliff.

Her walls pulsate around me as her body stiffens and she screams my name. There is nothing I love hearing more than the sound of her lost in bliss and calling out my fucking name. I follow her over the cliff, crashing as waves of pleasure run up my spine. My release spills into her, filling her.

I collapse next to her and pull her into my arms, bringing the blanket up to cover us. My fingers trail mindlessly up and down her back. We lie there in silence as we both let our breathing settle, our bodies relaxed. *Sated.*

"Josh, are you okay?" Emily's quiet voice breaks the silence. Am I okay? How the fuck do I answer that without depositing all of my stressors onto her? She doesn't deserve the burden of my worries.

"I will be," is the best answer I can come up with.

"Is there anything I can do to help?"

"You being here, that's helping more than you'll know. Don't worry, Em. All this shit will sort itself out." My lips meet the top of her head.

Her fingertips trace along her name branded on my chest. "I'm sorry," she whispers.

"You have nothing to be sorry for, Emmy. This isn't your fault."

"It is." She picks her head up and connects those blue eyes with mine. "Do you think I'm a horrible person?"

Her question shocks me. It makes me fucking angry to think she would even consider that. "Fuck no, I don't." My words come out harsher than I intended. Emily's eyes widen. She tries to push off me. Holding her tighter, I count to ten in my head. "Emmy, babe, you are literally the best thing since sliced bread. Actually, no, you're better. You are the best fucking thing on this whole planet. Why on earth would you think you're a horrible person?"

She shakes her head no. "I killed someone, Josh. I took a life from someone. And I'm not sorry. I don't feel bad about it. I should feel some sort of guilt. I should feel sorry, but I don't. The only thing I regret is that I didn't do it sooner. And I'm sorry that I've brought this burden to you. But I'm not sorry that I killed someone, and I should be, right? A normal person would feel something."

"Normal is overrated, Emmy. You are not normal. You are exceptional. Never aim to be normal, because normal is average, and trust me, babe, you are anything but average." I lean down, gently kissing her lips. "Also, you shouldn't feel sorry for defending yourself. You should feel fucking proud. I'm proud of you, Em. I'm not sorry that you came to me. I'm fucking ecstatic that you're here. You are not a burden. Don't you ever think that."

"I like having you back too. I wish it were under different circumstances. But I love you, Josh. I don't know what I'd do right now without you."

Maybe she's stopped thinking of her escape route. I feel like the last couple of weeks she's accepted the fact that we are an *us*. That she's not alone, but I still can't shake this sense of dread, this feeling that she wants to leave. Not that she wants to leave me, but the fact that she thinks she needs to protect me.

"I love you too. I don't want you to worry anymore, Em. Go to sleep. I'll be right here when you wake up."

"Okay." She lays her head back down on my chest.

I stare at the ceiling, not willing to close my eyes and let myself drift until after I feel her breathing slow, her body soften under my hands, her light little snores fill the room.

"FUCKING. Fuck. Fuck. Goddamn fucking shit piece of thing!" I yell as I throw my monitor across the room. It shatters, glass flying in every direction as it hits the wall.

I've been sitting in this office all fucking morning, going over every scrap of information my team has managed to uncover on Detective Jones. It's not fucking much. So far, we know he's a dirty fucking pig. He's recently been suspended. He's not even a fucking detective anymore. Whatever the fuck he wants with Emily has nothing to do with the law.

It's been three weeks. Three fucking weeks since I had to have Emily hauled up to my brother's house. She won't even leave the bedroom. I need to get this shit sorted, and sooner rather than later. Her words from a week ago replay back to me. *"Do you think I'm a horrible person?"* I've spent the last week trying to prove to her just how fucking perfect she is. The only problem is I've been spending more time here, in this fucking office, and out on the streets of Sydney than I have with her.

I've spent countless hours searching for any scrap of information on this fucker. He's like a goddamn ghost. He hasn't been seen since he questioned Dean at The Merge, the club my brother works security at. That doesn't mean he's disappeared. He's been sending daily emails directly to me. Each day, the threats get more detailed, more graphic. Today's email sent me over the edge, a red haze enveloping me.

Joshua,

You keep ignoring my messages. It would be wise for you to start listening. The longer it takes for me to get what I want, the worse it's going to be when I do get my hands on her. You know, I've heard all about that tight fucking cunt of hers. I've always wanted to see what all the fuss was about. Have you ever fucked a dead girl? You see, there's this moment when the fear overtakes them, and their cunts tighten to a painful point. That's when I'll slit her pretty little throat. I'll enjoy licking the tears from her cheeks, and when I do, you can drown in the knowledge she copped it worse because of you. Hand her over, and I might, just might, go easier on her.

DJ

IT TOOK Sam and three guys to hold me back when all I could think of was going on a fucking killing spree. He's got family. I've already found them. I have no issues in killing each fucking person off. He wants to threaten the one person I love. Let's see how he fucking likes it when I retaliate by doing the same. But I won't make fucking threats, and he won't see it coming until it's too fucking late.

Even with being held down by four grown fucking men, the only thing that dragged me out of that haze was my phone ringing with Emily's ringtone. She very rarely calls—today she called at the right time.

Now I'm sitting here, like a fucking useless fuck. He wants me to turn Emily over to him. He knows

I'm hiding her somewhere. But he will never get to her. I've already got us new identities, passports, bank accounts, and a plane fuelled and ready to go on a moment's notice. I will disappear with her if that's what it takes. There's a little island I purchased under a shell corporation. Nobody knows it exists—well, nobody but me.

I'm hoping it won't come to that. I want to give Emily everything she dreams of, the horses, the grandkids. *Everything*. I want to give her the fucking world. And I can't do that until I find this fucking asshole and deal with him.

Heading to the bar, I pour another glass of whisky, downing the contents as the door to my office gets thrown open. Sam walks in like he fucking owns the place. He helps himself to a glass before sitting on the lounger. He tilts his head at me, looking contemplative, then he speaks.

"Do you really think getting wasted at three in the afternoon is wise?" he asks.

"Got any better ideas?" I shrug as I pour another glass. Getting wasted seems like a really good bloody idea right now.

"Yeah, I do. Give me your keys. I'm driving. You're coming with me."

He stands, waiting for me to respond. "Where're we going?"

"Tony pinged the IP from the last email. It's a warehouse over in Marrickville, near Cooks River."

"Well, why didn't you fucking lead with that? Let's go." I swipe my keys and wallet off my desk and storm out of the office.

"Ah, you're not fucking driving, Josh. Give me the bloody keys." Sam steps in front of me at the lifts, holding his hand out. I only give him the keys because he's right. I can't drive right now. I'd probably end up driving us into the damn river at this point, not from being drunk, because I've only just started to get a light buzz on. No, I'd drive into the river out of pure fucking rage at this point.

I pass the keys over as the doors to the lift open. "Disregard any and all fucking road rules. Just get me to that warehouse."

"Done."

"WAIT, HOLD UP. ARE YOU CARRYING?" Sam stops me from jumping out of the car. We've pulled over at a block of abandoned industrial sheds. The place is deserted. For Sydney, that's fucking disturbing as hell. The thirty-minute trip gave me time to sober right up.

"Of course I am. And I'll be more than happy to

show you if you do not remove your hand, now!" I grit out. He knows I don't fucking like being touched, unless it's Emily doing the touching, that is. Thinking of Emily, I pull my phone out and send her a quick message.

Me: I'm taking you out for dinner. Be ready at seven.

Her response is immediate.

Emmy: I can't go to dinner, Josh. Let's just have dinner here.

Me: Em, we're going out. Be ready. Love you. xx

Emmy: Are you sure that's wise?

Me: Yes. Talk tonight. I gotta go.

Emmy: Okay.

Sliding my phone back into my pocket, I jump out of the car. Sam's waiting for me with a group of around ten men I'm assuming he's brought along. Walking up to the group, I instruct them, "If anyone sees this fucker, shoot to hurt, not kill. That kill is mine. Let's go."

I get a mixture of grunts and "yes, sirs" in response.

Sam leads the way to the warehouse marked number six. Pushing past him, I kick the door open. I pull the Glock out from my back and storm into the building.

"Jesus Christ, Josh, let the whole fucking neighbourhood know we're here, why don't you."

"Shut up!" I hiss. I stop and listen. I identify and dismiss each distant sound: the wind rattling tin against tin, the dripping pipes, scurrying animals. There's nothing else. This building is fucking empty. Or the fucker's already a rotting corpse, because it sure does fucking stink like decay in here.

It's dark, apart from the light streaming in from the door we just kicked down. There're no windows in here. Looking around, I see a switch on the wall. When I pull the lever down, the warehouse lights up.

As soon as the lights come on, I see the reason why it stinks like rotting corpses. I look back at Sam. His face is pale, a few guys behind him already leaning over and losing the contents of their stomachs.

What the fuck did we just walk into? I can't help but feel like this is a setup, somehow. "Nobody touch a fucking thing," I say as I step further into the room. The sight before me is enough to give the fucking devil nightmares. It's a damn good thing I don't fucking scare easily.

There are three bodies, three female bodies. These women have been brutally tortured; ripped clothing hangs from their rotting flesh. As I inspect closer, my skin crawls. All three women have long blonde hair, their vacant blue eyes open and damning. I feel like they're staring right at me… accusingly. I didn't get here sooner. I haven't caught the bastard before he could do this to these women. The part that disturbs me the most is they all look like Emily.

This could be Emily's lifeless body lying here. Fuck! Turning around, I'm about to walk out when I spot the far wall. Sam's already over there taking photos with his phone of everything on display. As I walk up next to him, my hands are shaking. Spread out all over the wall are images of Emily. Old ones, and more recent ones of her at my apartment and out at the ranch.

How long has this fucker been watching her? There's image after image of her beaten and bruised, a few with casts on her arm. There're images of her spread out on a bed, naked, bruises and cuts all over her body. My gun drops to the ground, the sound echoing in the otherwise silent room.

I start tearing at the images, ripping them from the wall. I don't stop until every single one is in shreds. Once I'm satisfied that every photo is destroyed, I bend down, pick up my gun and walk out.

"Torch the fucking place," I grunt as I walk past

the men standing at the entrance watching, waiting and unsure what the fuck to do.

I need to get home to Emily. I need to hold her living, breathing body in my arms. I need to breathe in her fruity scent, feel the pulse in her neck beneath my hand. This fucking prick of an ex-detective is going to have one hell of a fight on his hands if he thinks I'll ever let him get even an inch near her. I should have fucking shot his ass back on the side of the road when the asshole had the audacity to pull up behind me and question me about Emily.

CHAPTER 10

EMILY

I'm not sure why I'm so nervous. It's Josh. I'm going out to dinner with Josh. Why the hell am I so nervous? Argh, I wipe my sweaty palms down the fabric of my dress, then recoil at the thought of possibly marking what has to be the softest freaking fabric I've ever worn.

I went in search of Ella's help as soon as Josh texted and asked me to be ready for dinner. Okay, well, he didn't ask so much as tell. But, again, it's Josh. I'm sure if I put my foot down, and really expressed how much I'd rather stay home, he wouldn't push it. He would let me stay here. Argh, why can't I just be normal?

Because normal is overrated and average. I hear Josh's voice repeating those words to me, like he has every day this past week. I just need to calm down. Looking at my reflection in the floor-length mirror, I let out the breath I've been holding. I don't know what Ella did, other than wave some bloody magic wand over me, because I don't look like the plain old Emily right now.

I'm wearing a knee-length black cocktail dress. It has a squared neckline, my breasts popping out the top, with probably way too much cleavage on display. The dress is tight, like painted on my body kind of tight. And there is a slit that runs right up the front of my left leg, stopping about two inches from my hip bone.

My hair is loosely curled, falling down my back. My face though… I don't know what she's done, but my eyes look three times bigger than usual, the blue really popping against the gold-toned eyeshadows. And my lips, fire-engine red. This girl looking back at me is not me. She's beautiful. I almost feel like I've got a disguise on. I'm not used to seeing myself look like this. I'm also not used to wearing dresses this nice.

I don't know how I'm meant to walk around without flashing everyone the black lace panties I have on underneath the dress. That's if I don't fall and break an ankle in the black strappy stilettos Ella had me put on. I tried to argue that I wouldn't be able to walk in them. Her response was: *"You'll have Josh to lean on anyway. You know that boy's not gonna let you fall flat on your face."*

The shoes do look really good, and I love how my legs look in them. I am, however, self-conscious of how much skin I have showing right now. What is Josh going to say when he sees me? I don't even know where we are going. What if this dress is too much? I mean, what if he just wanted to take me to McDonald's?

Shaking my hands out in an attempt to ease my nerves, I eye that bar fridge I've not inspected yet. Maybe if I just drink a little something, I can calm down enough to at least pretend to be normal.

I'm bending at the waist to examine the insides of the fridge, because this dress is too tight to bend down any other way. The fridge is filled with tiny bottles, most of which I don't recognise. The two bottles I do recognise are a sweet white wine or champagne. I opt for the bottle of sweet bubbly white.

"You know, I'm tempted to skip dinner and head straight into dessert, with that ass of yours being the only thing on my menu."

I jump out of my skin, straightening up and spinning around, only to slam into Josh's chest. Josh's very naked chest. Very wet, naked chest. Tiny water droplets drip down his torso. The moan involuntarily slips out of my lips.

"Fuck, Emmy, are you trying to give me a heart attack. Because damn, you look incredible." Josh takes the bottle from my hands. Stepping back, he twists the top off before holding the bottle back out to me. His eyes rake up and down my body.

"Thank you." My voice is just as shaky as my hands when I take the drink back and bring the bottle to my mouth. Why the hell am I so twisted about whether or not he likes the dress? I don't care what he thinks about it. I like it and that's all that matters. The lie I'm telling myself isn't working. I do care what he thinks and it's pissing me off, because I know I shouldn't.

Josh stares at my shaky hands. "What's wrong?"

"Nothing," I lie.

"Emmy, I fucking love you. But you're a shit-ass liar. Now, what's wrong?" he says, more persistent.

"I am not a shit-ass liar. When I was fourteen, I had my dad believe I was at a sleepover at my friend Katie's. When really, I went to..." I snap my mouth shut. That is not a story for Josh's ears. That's one of those I'll take it to my grave stories and never tell a soul.

"When you were really what? Go on, finish the sentence. This, I can't wait to hear."

"It doesn't matter. The moral of the story is: if I could get away with lying to my dad, who was a trained special forces soldier, then I think I'm a pretty good liar." I shrug.

"Emmy, I'm aware who your father was and what he did. But I'd love to know what it was you were really doing while you were supposed to be at your friend Katie's? That sounds like a story I should know. Also, we don't keep secrets from each other. Spill the beans, Em." He smirks.

Well, let's see how long he's wearing that cocky grin when I tell him what I was really doing that night I *didn't* stay at Katie's. "Okay, if you're so insistent on knowing, I'll tell you." I crook my finger at him, ushering him closer so I can whisper. Leaning into his ear, I tell him, "I went to the movies with Carter. He was the captain of our school's swim team. Real fast, he was. We sat up in the back of the theatre and..."

My sentence is cut off. Sparks explode throughout my body as Josh's lips smash against mine. His kiss has a way of making me lose all sense of reality. When Josh kisses me, everything in the room fades away, my senses overridden by my body's reaction to his.

"Mmm, I missed you," I mumble as I break away from his lips, fisting his shirt in one hand and trying not to drop my tiny wine bottle that's grasped in my other.

"I missed you more."

"Not a competition. Want the rest of that story now?" I ask sweetly.

"Nope, I'm going to be with your dad on this one and pretend that you really did stay at Katie's house all night."

"Okay." I step back, sipping on the wine. The sweet, fruity taste lingers on my tongue.

"Now, tell me what's wrong?" Josh says. Damn it, I thought he'd forgotten about that.

"It's nothing. Where are we going tonight anyway?"

"Emmy, it's not nothing. I can tell something's on your mind. I can't fix it for you if you don't tell me."

"You know you can't fix everything, right?"

"Try me?"

"Oh my God, you're relentless. Okay, I'm freaking out. Are you happy? I don't know where the bloody hell you're taking me. I don't know what I'm supposed to do. I don't know what I'm supposed to wear. If I look okay or not. If you like my dress, if it's too much... not enough? I don't know what the rules are. How am I supposed to keep to the rules if I don't know them?"

I'm yelling by the time I finish my tirade. I look up to see Josh's blank face. Great, he's got the *I'm not giving you an expression* face on. I hate that face. I can't read that face. I'm trying to replay what I just said to him in my head. Did I say something I shouldn't have?

Instinctively, I take a step to the side, trying to make space between us. The moment I do, that's when I see a tiny flicker of emotion in his eyes. He's annoyed. That's a look I know well. It's just not usually directed at me.

I wait him out. I don't know what to say or do after my little outburst. So, I just stand here and wait, like a deer caught in the headlights. Josh holds up his hand, all five fingers pointed up in the air.

"First, when it comes to you, I will always be relentless." He puts one finger down.

"Second, no, I'm not happy. I'm not happy because I can clearly see that you're not. I can't be happy when you're not okay, Em. I won't be happy until you are." He releases a breath.

"Third, I was planning to take you to a nice restaurant, have dinner, candles and shit. But I've had a change of plans. I'm taking you to The Merge.

We are going to let our hair down and let loose." He puts another finger down.

"Fourth, you are fucking stunning in anything you wear. Whatever you choose to wear is the *right* thing. I cannot tell you enough how much I fucking love that dress on you. But if you hate it, then I hate it too. I want you to dress for you, Emmy, not anyone else." Another finger goes down. All I can do is stand here and nod an acknowledgement.

"And Fifth... Rules? There are no rules, Emmy. You are the fucking queen of the McKinley Empire; you make the fucking rules. Do not, and I repeat, do not let any other fuckers try to tell you any differently."

I don't even know what to say. That is a lot to take in, the power he is giving me, the control to make my own choices. As much as I want to be able to do all the things he says I can do, make my own decisions, my own rules, I'm afraid I don't know how to be that girl anymore. There's a constant bit of doubt that lingers in the back of my head, telling me it's just a trick, mind games.

What I can do is pretend. I've been getting better at pretending these last few weeks. I just need to keep doing it. I plaster a smile on my face, straighten my shoulders and fake the confidence that I don't yet have.

"We're going to the club Ella works at?" I ask excitedly. At least the enthusiasm is real. I've heard so much about The Merge. I've been wanting to go and see it for myself. According to Ella, it's the hottest club in Sydney, not that I would know. It's been years since I've been out, anywhere, let alone a nightclub.

Josh smirks and looks me up and down. "We are. But if you'd prefer, we can go to dinner."

"Are you kidding me? I want to see this fancy nightclub I keep hearing about. Are you sure I look okay for that?" I ask, glancing down at my dress again.

"You look perfect. You are perfect. Now, let's go." Josh holds his arm out, indicating for me to go in front of him.

"Fuck, Jesus Christ to all that is holy." He groans. I turn around, confused.

"What's wrong?" I ask.

"Hold on a sec. I just need to grab something real quick." Josh walks into his closet. Moments later, he walks back out, wearing a shoulder holster over his dress shirt. He stops at a chest of drawers and pulls out what looks like a small armoury. He selects two handguns, securing them into the holster.

"Why do you need those?" I ask as he makes his

way back over to me while throwing a jacket on. We're only going to a nightclub.

"Babe, have you seen your ass in that dress? Every man in that place is going to have their eyes on you."

My eyebrows rise to my hairline. "You're joking, right? Josh, you can't go around shooting people. Even if they did look at me, which I doubt they will, but if they did, you cannot shoot people in Ella's club. It'll leave a mess."

"I'll pay for the cleaning bill." He laughs as he leads me out of the room with his hand on the small of my back.

CHAPTER 11

JOSH

Stopping at the valet out front of The Merge, I turn to look at Emily. "Wait for me to open your door."

I jump out and hand the keys to the guy waiting. "You scratch it, I'll repaint the whole car with your blood." I smile at him. He stands there with his mouth hanging open as I jog around to the other side to let Emily out.

I have to stand directly in front of her while she manoeuvres herself from the car. I wasn't about to let every fucker get a glimpse of those black lace panties I just saw. I have to readjust myself in my pants. I'm a walking fucking hard-on right now—

have been ever since I saw her bent over the bar fridge back in our room.

Emmy's grip on my hand tightens as she looks around the crowd currently lined up to get into the club. I pull her into my side, wrapping my arm around her shoulder. Leaning into her neck, I whisper, "The moment you feel like you need to leave, tell me and I'll get you out."

She nods her head, then puts that fake fucking smile back on her face. The same one she's been wearing for a few weeks now. I can always tell the difference (most people can't). But I know the one she's wearing right now is fake as hell. I haven't called her out on it though.

If she needs a mask to hide beneath, then I'll let her. Right now, she's handling whatever inner demons she's carrying around the way she needs to. If she can't handle it anymore, then she'll have me to handle it for her. Until then, I'll be here as her backup.

I walk us straight up to the door, bypassing the waiting patrons attempting to get in. Security pulls the rope aside the moment they spot me.

"Good evening, Mr. McKinley," one greets as he opens the door, at which, Emily giggles next to me. A real giggle, not a fake one.

"Something amusing?" I ask her.

"Just the whole Mr. McKinley thing. It makes you sound old. Wait, oh my gosh, is that a grey hair?" She reaches up, running her fingers through the front of my hair.

"It's blonde, not fucking grey. Also, we're exactly the same age, babe. If I'm old, what does that make you?"

She laughs. "Good point. We can be old together."

I'm leading her straight to the stairs for the VIP area when she just stops. I glance over at her. Her eyes are wide and her head turns, looking in every direction of the club.

I try to see the place the way she might. The walls are lined with red velvet curtains. Three stories high. The top two have balconies, which overlook the huge dance area on the ground floor where we are standing now. There's sectioned-off seating with a variety of bench seats and sofas. There are bar tables and coffee tables—all have a collection of gold sculpted bodies that are merged together in different kinds of erotic positions capped with a glass tabletop.

There's a main bar that runs along one side of the floor; it's already packed with people waiting to order their next rounds. Thank fuck we don't have to line up like that.

"You good?" I lean into Emily so she can hear me

over the sound of the music. Her face lights up; a genuine smile greets me.

"This is amazingly beautiful," she yells out.

"I'll be sure to tell the owner," a gravelly voice says from behind us. I turn around, placing myself in front of Emmy and coming face to face with Zac. My brother's best friend. And the owner of this club. There's no love lost between us. We tolerate each other, for Dean's sake. Now, more for Ella's sake, considering this asshole is my new sister-in-law's brother. I don't even know where the hostility between us started. Maybe it's just always been there. I've honestly never cared to try to work it out.

"Zac." I nod my head at him. If he expects anything more, then he can fuck right off.

"Josh. I trust you're not going to go off on a crazy rampage and leave my club looking like a blood bath tonight?" He smirks.

Emily shoves herself in front of me. Where the hell she found the strength to move me, I don't know. It's probably because she caught me off guard. That's what I'll go with. She stands there with her arms crossed over her chest, her breasts popping out of the top of her dress even more. They look fucking delicious.

One thing I'll give Zac, his eyes never waver from her face. His amused smirk though, that pisses me off. I can tell it's having the same effect on Emily. I decide not to step in, and to let her handle this. I'm intrigued as to what she'll do.

"Zac, the only reason you still have your balls attached to your body right now is because I happen to like your wife. *But* I won't warn you again, if you call Josh crazy or make any comment to suggest that he is, I will cut them off. I'll make meatballs out of them and feed them to his pigs. I've heard they particularly like chewing on the balls of assholes."

Fuck me. My boner just got ten times harder. She's fucking hot as hell when she speaks her mind. Zac, however, covers his balls with his hand. He screws his face up in disgust before he starts laughing.

"I'll have to thank my wife for being so damn lovable. Come on, I've got you two lovebirds a table upstairs."

I wrap an arm around Emmy's waist, holding her in place. "We'll be up in a moment." Zac walks away, shaking his head. As soon as he's out of sight, Emmy spins around.

"Oh God, Josh, I'm so sorry. I didn't mean to. I just… I don't know what comes over me. I hate when people try to say you're crazy. It's not okay and I just… God, I'm sorry."

"Don't be sorry. *I'm not.* I'm fucking hard as a

damn steel pole right now." I press my cock into her stomach so she can feel exactly what I'm talking about.

"The idea of pigs eating balls turns you on, huh?" She smirks.

I shiver at the image. "Fuck no. *You* turn me on. When you speak your mind, that shit's a fucking turn-on. When you stand up for me, which by the way you really do not need to do, that's a fucking turn-on. A complete other level of turn-on." I look around. There's gotta be a bathroom around here somewhere. A closet? Office? Fuck, I'll take a dark corner at this point.

"Uh, thanks? I think. What are you looking for?"

"Somewhere I can take you and fuck you where no one else will see what's mine. You heard Zac. He doesn't want his club to be a blood bath tonight, which means no fucker can see your face when I make you come. Otherwise, I'll have to shoot them."

"Wow, okay. Um, how about we file that idea for when we get back to your place. Because as appealing as that is, I kind of wanna see what's upstairs. Come on."

Emily grabs my hand and leads the way, following the path she watched Zac take. Pulling her back into me, I wrap an arm around her shoulder. "*Our* place. And I'm not sure I can wait that long. My balls are literally aching right now, Emmy."

"You'll survive. Delayed gratification and all." She laughs.

"SAM, YOU'RE HERE." Emily jumps up, throwing her arms around him a few too many drinks later. Sam holds his arms out to his side, staring straight at me and not returning her hug. That is, until he realises she ain't gonna let go unless he does. He lightly pats her back and pulls her arms from around his neck.

"You're seriously trying to get me killed, Emily. You know that, right?" he says to her.

"Stop it. He's not allowed to shoot anyone tonight. Zac said so."

Sam's eyebrows rise as he laughs. "That fucker is too crazy to listen to reason. If he wanted to shoot me, he would. Fuck, he'd probably even do it in a damn church."

The next thing I see is Sam hunched over, grabbing hold of his balls, right where Emily's knee just slammed into him. I wince for him. Even if he deserved it, that shit fucking hurts like hell.

"You know what? Zac said Josh couldn't shoot anyone. He didn't say *I* couldn't. Josh, hand me a gun." Emily holds her hand out behind her in my direction.

As much as I want to hand her a gun and see what she actually does with it, I also don't want my friend shot tonight.

"Babe, if I can't shoot anyone, then neither can you. Also, you're drunk. You won't even be able to aim properly." I laugh, pulling her down onto my lap.

"I wouldn't miss. I bet I'm the best shot here out of all of you," she says, pointing to each of the men at the table. As soon as Emily and I sat down, it seemed Ella's whole fucking tribe came and crashed our party. Ella, I don't mind so much. She doesn't piss me off every other second. Dean, Bray, Zac and their wives though? Different story. Actually, Alyssa is sweet as hell. Even I can't not like her. Reilly, Bray's wife... that chick is crazier than me. I feel like I always have to be on high alert when she's around.

"Okay, Little Miss Sniper. How much we putting on this? I'm in. There's no way you're a better shot than me," Bray asks Emily.

I've actually never heard if she can shoot or not. But my money will always be on her. I don't even care if I win or lose. Because as long as I have her, I'm already winning.

"One mil?" I offer up a bet, waiting for Bray to either counter or back out.

Emily gasps. She turns and whispers in my ear, "Josh, I don't have one mil. What if I lose?"

"Babe, how confident are you that you can beat him?" I ask her.

She looks over at him, then turns back to me and smiles. "Extremely." She nods.

I don't know if it's the alcohol in her system or not, but I'm not about to let her lose that confidence. "Make it two million," I tell Bray.

He laughs. "Sure, if you wanna throw your fancy McKinley money away, who am I to say no?" he asks.

"Ah, Bray, that's a lot of freaking money. What if you lose?" Reilly asks.

"Rye, relax, there's no way I'm losing. Besides, I married a trust fund brat. I'm good for it." He laughs and dodges her strike.

I've read about Reilly's family. Her dad was a big-time investor before he went to jail; he left her and her twin (Holly) a hefty little nest egg. Not that Bray needs her money, these fuckers have more cash than they know what to do with. Maybe it's not the McKinley kind of money, but they're a long way from begging.

"Josh, this is crazy. You can't waste that much money. What if I lose?" Emily asks again.

"I don't actually care if you win or lose. It'll be fun to watch him sweat a bit. He's far too cocky.

"I'll do my best," she says.

"Babe, relax." Whispering in her ear, I tell her, "We make over a million dollars in one day. We can afford to lose a couple." Her eyes widen.

"*You* make that, Josh. Not me. I'm homeless. I don't even have a job. I didn't even get to finish university. I'm probably never going to get a job."

"You know you're never going to need a job, Em, but if you want to do something, I'll do whatever I can to make sure you can do it."

"I don't think I can go back to school now. It's been too many years."

"You can do whatever you want."

"We'll see."

"Emmy, people go to Uni at all ages. If you want to go back to med school, I can make sure you get into the best school in Australia."

"How'd you know I was in med school?"

I look over to Sam. "He found your records. Not that I was surprised. You're the smartest person I know."

"No, I'm not. But I do need to pee. I'll be back." She goes to get off my lap.

"I'll come with you."

"You are not coming to the bathroom with me, Joshua. Sit down." She folds her arms over her chest.

"Fine, Ella, go with Emily." Ella doesn't argue; she

stands up and links arms with my girl. I nod to the security guy sitting at the bar watching, instructing him to follow.

"You know she's not going to disappear into thin air, right?" Bray laughs.

"Fuck off."

"Just saying. You also don't have x-ray vision, so no matter how much you stare at the wall, you won't be able to see her."

He's fucking right. I can't see her anymore and it makes my skin crawl. I don't like it. I feel like something's wrong. Like I should have gone with her.

I try to shake the feeling and down the glass of whisky Dean puts in front of me.

"Josh, you good?" Sam asks.

"Yeah, fine."

"No, you're not."

"You're right. I'm not." I get up and head in the direction Emily went. Something in my gut is telling me I need to find her. I always fucking trust my gut.

CHAPTER 12

EMILY

"Wow!" I don't think I've ever been in a nightclub bathroom this fancy. The floors and walls are covered in white marble tiles. There is a chandelier—a huge, blingy chandelier—in the middle of the room. There's a row of vanity tables with pink fluffy stools. This must be how the other half lives.

"Yeah, I had it redecorated to be more feminine," Ella says as she takes in the bathroom.

"I'm almost too afraid to pee in here. It's too nice." I laugh.

Just then, Ella's phone starts blaring. "Go pee. I'm just gonna step outside and take this."

I nod and head into the stall. I can hear the sound of heels clicking on the tiles as I finish up, straighten my dress and flush the loo. I head out to the basin. Just before I reach the sink, I'm yanked back by my hair. My whole body freezes. My eyes shut. I can't open them. He's found me. He's not dead; he's here.

My body drops to the floor. "You stupid fucking bitch. You ruined everything." A high-pitched squeal echoes through the room. That's a female's voice; that's not him. It's not him. I'm okay. Well, I will be once I get off this damn floor.

I open my eyes just in time to see the hand flying towards my face and landing with a sharp sting. I smile at her. If that's her worst, she's about to be really bloody sorry for hitting me. I want to know what it is I ruined though. So, before I retaliate, I ask her, "Do I know you?"

I know exactly who she is. She's the stupid bitch who was at Josh's penthouse a few weeks ago. But the look that crosses her face is priceless.

"I'm the future Mrs. Joshua McKinley, bitch. He. Is. Mine. I know he was almost ready to pop the question before you came on the scene."

I think she's delusional. There is no way Josh would consider marrying someone like her. The thought that he even slept with her is disturbing enough. "Look, clearly you've let Josh fuck you. So, I'm sure you know that he has a name inked across his heart. That's my name, idiot. He was never yours." I push her off me and sit up. "He will never be yours."

"That's where you're wrong. I don't care what name he has on his skin. It will be my name on that marriage certificate. *That's* all that matters." She stands up and opens the little clutch she's holding, pulling out a knife.

Well, that puts a damper on my night. How do I get myself out of here? I look to the door and she steps in front of me.

"No one's coming to help you. You won't be walking out of this bathroom." She leans down into my face. Holding the knife at my throat, she says, "I'm going to enjoy fucking you out of his system." Then, as if on cue, the door slams open and Josh storms in.

Without a word, he effortlessly picks Whitney up. "I thought I warned you about going anywhere near Emily."

"Josh, she attacked me. Don't let her do this to us." Josh laughs, before his face becomes passive. Blank.

"You should have stayed away," he says as he grabs the knife out of her hands and slices it right across her throat. She lets out a gurgled sound, and then nothing. The room goes silent.

I can't stop the gasp that comes out. I've never seen anything so graphically violent, aside from my own beatings… and what I did to Trent. But those instances were different… the memories are blurred. Frenzied. I wasn't in the background, witnessing everything like I am now. Josh looks at me. "Fuck." He drops her body, stepping over her. There's blood, so much blood. It's the only thing I can focus on. The blood pooling around her neck…

"Emmy, I'm sorry. I shouldn't have done that in front of you." Josh squats down on the floor next to me.

He shouldn't have done that *at all*. I know that. It's on the tip of my tongue to say. I should say it. But I can't, even though I know what he's done is wrong. I also know what I've done is wrong. I can't look at him and not still be completely and utterly in love with him. Is this what crazy is? I know they say love is blind, but this is beyond that.

"Josh, we need to clean this mess up. Zac said no blood baths, remember? That kinda looks like a blood bath." I nod my head to the body, now limp and framed in red.

"Yeah, babe, don't worry about it. Are you okay? Are you hurt?"

I shake my head no. I'm not hurt. "I'm okay. Are… are you okay?" I ask him.

"I'm fine. Emmy, can I pick you up?"

Why is he asking to pick me up? It dawns on me that he hasn't touched me at all. He's just been sitting in front of me. I nod my head yes. Josh picks me up and settles me on the vanity bench. His hand comes up and brushes my hair away from my face.

"Fuck. Shit. Don't move. Let me clean that." He reaches for a towel from the pile sitting on the bench opposite us. My hands grab his shirt, and I pull him back to me. My lips find his. I lose myself in this kiss, in him. This is what I need. I need him.

He kisses me back tentatively at first, keeping his hands away from me. I need him to touch me. I know it's all kinds of fucked up. I should be disgusted right now. I should be running for the damn hills. But this is the man my soul connects with on such a deep level. Right now, I need to feel our connection more than anything, and he's holding back. I don't know why. He's never held back like this before.

I wrap my legs around his waist and pull him in closer. I can feel the hardness of his cock against my centre. Moaning into his mouth, I rub myself on him. Something snaps in Josh in that exact moment. His hands go straight for my hair, tilting my head back and angling my mouth at a slant that gives him a deeper vantage point. His tongue duels with mine as we both fight for control of the kiss.

Josh trails one hand down my back, pulling me closer to him as he grinds on me. I'm wet, the lace of my panties doing nothing to contain my arousal. I can feel my excitement sticking to my inner thighs.

"Mmm, Josh, I need you," I murmur into his mouth. His response is to growl, biting down on my lower lip.

"What the fuck, Josh!" I hear yelled at us. I'm too drunk on this kiss to even care who it is. I want more. I need more of Josh, and whoever just walked in has interrupted.

Josh breaks away from the kiss, while attempting to pull my dress down my thighs to a respectable level. When he realises it's not going to happen, he gives up and lifts me from the bench, fixing my hem before he turns around.

"Sorry?" he questions both Dean and Sam, who are standing in the bathroom looking down at a lifeless body. Both of whom don't seem too fussed with the scene. More annoyed.

"Sorry… you're sorry? What the fuck happened in here? Emily, are you okay, sweetheart?" Dean asks.

Huh, interesting. I've always had a feeling that he

didn't like me very much. Yet he always asks if I'm okay. I nod my head and step in front of Josh. I will not let anyone give him a hard time about helping me. Protecting me.

"I'm sorry. It's my fault. She came at me with a knife and I freaked out. By the time Josh came in here, she was already dead." The lie easily slips from my mouth—a lie I will repeat over and over if it means protecting Josh from any fallout from this.

"Holy shit, Em. I take back what I said about you being a shitty liar, because that was fucking gold." Josh laughs from behind me.

"Josh, not the time for that conversation," I hiss out.

"Jesus, you've got it bad, girl." Sam shakes his head. "Blink once if you need rescuing," he tells me.

I raise my eyebrows at him and tilt my head. "How are your balls feeling, Sam?"

"Yep, that's my cue to arrange a clean-up crew. Be right back. Don't leave this bathroom, kids. You both look like shit. Well, not you, Emily. You could never look like shit." Sam winks as he exits the room.

"Emily, don't ever lie for Josh again. He's a big boy and can definitely clean up his own mess," Dean says pointedly to me before directing at Josh, "And you, really? Why is it every time you come here, you leave a mess behind?"

"That's an exaggeration, Dean. You would have done the same thing. She had a knife at Emmy's throat when I came in here. Tell me you wouldn't have done the same thing for Ella." Josh takes hold of my hand. I can feel the trembling. I squeeze tight and hold on. This is a sign he's about to lose his shit. I need him to calm down.

"Of course I would have. I would have done the same for Emily too, you know. I'm not saying you did the wrong thing, just really shitty fucking timing."

"Oh my God!" Ella screeches from the doorway before her pale face looks up at us.

"Fucking hell. El, Princess, calm down." Dean wraps his arms around her.

"Calm down, Dean? There's a dead girl in my bathroom and you're telling me to calm down." Her voice rises even louder when two more men come through the door.

"Jesus Christ, Josh, I thought I told you no blood tonight." Zac curses as he looks from the body to me and Josh.

"It wasn't Josh. It was me. It's my fault. I did it," I say, folding my arms over my chest. Zac and Bray both burst out laughing. I square my shoulders.

"What's so funny about that?" I ask.

"She's a keeper, that one, Josh." Bray smirks.

"Ella, you good?" Zac asks, turning to his sister.

"I'd be better with less blood around. Dean, I need a drink, now!" Ella stomps out of the bathroom. I feel bad. She was so proud of how nice this bathroom was, and I've ruined it.

"Emily, are you okay?" Zac asks me. I'm a little shocked. He hasn't really said much all night. He mostly sits there, looking grouchy and staring at wherever Alyssa is.

"Uh, yep. I think so," I answer.

"I'm okay too. Thanks for asking," Josh says. "Sam will have a clean-up crew here in no time. Don't worry, you won't even know they were here."

"Yeah, I think I'll organise my own. Bray, call them in. I want this bathroom remodelled. *Again*. Follow me. There's a bathroom in my office you two can use."

Zac walks out. "Wow, you must have made a good impression, Emily. He won't even let me use his bloody bathroom," Bray says while typing away on his phone.

It dawns on me that no one, not a single one of these men were deterred by the fact that there is a body surrounded by blood on the floor right now.

"Is Zac like a mafia boss or something? Because I get that, you know, it's only family blah blah, but that's probably something someone should have told me before I threatened to feed his balls to the pigs," I question both Josh and Bray.

"Wait, you what? Seriously, what is it with you two and those fucking pigs? It's fucking gross."

"Babe, he is not mafia. You read way too many books." Josh laughs as he pulls me out of the room.

We make it up to Zac's office easily enough. "Bathroom's through there. I'll be downstairs. Try not to kill anyone," Zac grunts as he walks out.

"Sure thing," Josh says, leading me into the bathroom and closing the door behind him. I find myself in yet another over-the-top, luxurious bathroom. Josh is silent as he turns the water on, adjusting the tap until he's satisfied with the temperature.

He's also silent as he removes his jacket, then his holster and shirt. His eyes never leave mine as he toes off his shoes and pulls his pants down. I just stand here. As I wait in the silence, the whole scene of what just happened replays in my head. In graphic detail. The dead look in Josh's eyes as he ran the knife across her throat. My reaction afterwards. All the blood…

I feel nauseous. My body erupts in a cold sweat, causing me to shiver. Oh God, I'm going to be sick. Rushing to the loo, I crouch down over it. Can my life get any more miserable right now? Tears stream down my cheeks as my stomach rejects every bit of liquor I've consumed tonight. My whole body shakes as I sob into the porcelain bowl.

Josh is right behind me, rubbing his hand up and down my back, holding my hair away from my face and whispering how everything is going to be all right. He's wrong. How is it going to be all right? How can we ever be okay? We're both fucked up. Josh and I are two very messed up wrongs. They say two wrongs do not make a right. If that's true, then why does being *his* feel so damn right?

"Emmy, babe, it's going to be okay. We are going to be okay. We have to be."

"Josh, what's wrong with me?" I ask him.

"Em, you're in shock. It's okay. That… I shouldn't have done that in front of you. I will never forgive myself for that. I'm sorry, so fucking sorry."

"That's the thing, Josh. I should care. I should be running right now. Except I don't care. I don't care that I just watched you… you… I don't care about *that*. I should care, but I don't. That's not normal. Love shouldn't be so blind. We shouldn't be okay with this."

"Emily, look at me." The fact that he called me Emily makes my head snap right up. He rarely calls me Emily. It's always Emmy or Em.

"There is nothing wrong with you. There is nothing wrong with *us*. What we have, it's so much more than love, Emily. What we have, the connection we share, it's unbreakable. It always has been. We have something people spend their whole lives wishing to find. The stuff Hallmark wished they could capture in a card. What we have, whatever it is, it's beautiful. It's extraordinary. Immeasurable. It's unfailing."

Josh kisses the top of my head and lifts me up to my feet. He unzips my dress, slowly pulling it down my body. He bends over and unclips my shoes, removing one at a time before dragging my panties down my legs.

I capture my reflection in the mirror. My hair stained with blood from Josh's hands. My eyes red. My face blotchy. And all I can think is: *I've looked worse.*

CHAPTER 13

JOSH

I've been lying here for hours, replaying the events of the night. Emily cried herself to sleep in my arms. Her rest has been unsettled, plagued with constant stirring. My hand mindlessly runs up and down her back in attempts to soothe her, to calm her. For the first time, I'm guilt-ridden after ending another's life.

I'm not sorry for killing Whitney. The bitch deserved it. No, I don't feel guilty over her. I feel like shit because I lost control and let Emily see me do something so horrendous. It's one thing for her to know I'm capable or even willing to do such a thing, but it's completely different for her to witness me in the act.

I'm shocked she's still here. I'm so afraid that she's going to wake up and what I did will suddenly sink in. She's going to see how too-fucking-good for me she is, and she's going to want to disappear again. I've never been afraid of anything like I am of losing Emily, of having her fear me.

I've made so much progress with getting her to trust in me. To trust that I'm not ever going to hurt her like she has been. How can I expect her to trust that fact after what she saw?

It's almost dawn. I'm running on no sleep and I have to go into the fucking office in two hours. I haven't told Emily about the emails or threats.

Until yesterday, I didn't think too much of them. They were disturbing and fucking pissed me off. It wasn't until I saw the evidence left behind of what that sick fuck is capable of that I got scared. That I grasped how real the threat to Emily is. How am I meant to leave her side, knowing that some sick fucker is out to get her? Knowing exactly what he will do if he does get to her?

What I don't understand is the why. Why the fuck is he so hell-bent on getting his hands on Emily? The sooner I pinpoint the connection and determine what he wants, the sooner I can plan how to draw him out and erase the fucking prick.

"Mmm, did you sleep at all?" I look down into the depths of Emily's blue eyes staring up at me.

"A little," I lie.

"I'm sorry. I don't know how to tell you how sorry I am," she says. I wish she would get it through her head that she doesn't need to be fucking sorry for shit.

"Emmy, you have nothing to apologize for." Leaning down, I connect my lips with hers. The moment I do, all my worries get pushed to the back of my mind, my thoughts clear. The only focus is the feel of Emily's soft, plump lips on mine. The sparks that ignite throughout my body. Her scent all around me. I drown in all that is Emily as soon as our lips connect.

Emily pulls away from the kiss. I can't help but pout at her. I want those delicious lips. "I'm sorry for what you had to do to protect me. I'm sorry I've brought so much trouble into your life. It was never my intention."

"Emmy, I fucking love you. So damn much. There is nothing I wouldn't do to protect you. There is no one I wouldn't slay to ensure your safety. Fuck, even God will have a damn fight on his hands when he tries to claim his angel back. Because I guarantee you: I am one devil who won't give up on you."

"Ah, pretty sure my chances of heaven have long since passed. Don't worry, we'll both be going to the same place."

"Babe, you haven't done a damn thing wrong. You are an innocent survivor, who fought her demons and won."

"Then why doesn't it feel like I've won? He's winning even now. His death hasn't stopped my hell. I'm still hiding out. I'm still running. I just want it to be over, Josh. I'm tired of being scared."

"It will be over soon, Emmy. I promise. And then, you and I are getting that white picket fence. We're going to fill stables with horses. We'll have dogs, cats, sheep, chickens… Fuck, I'll get you a damn alpaca if you want one. We are going to have the future you've always dreamt of. The future I've always dreamt of."

"I hope you're right."

"Haven't you heard? I'm always right."

Emily's laughter feeds my soul, illuminating the sombre mood we were both in. Her joy is the best medicine. And it's contagious. I want to hear it all damn day.

"Babe, get up. Put on some swimmers and a sundress. Pack a hat and sun lotion. We're going out for the day." I roll her off me and jump out of bed with a sudden burst of energy. I've just decided that Emily and I are spending the entire day together. It's my mission to hear that laugh of hers for the duration.

"Where are we going? Don't you have to go to work?" I can feel her eyes on my naked ass as I make my way into the closet. Turning, I catch her checking me out.

"Em, my eyes are up here." I smirk, pointing to my face.

"I know, but that ass, Josh. It deserves attention." She laughs.

"Fair call. We are going everywhere. Ever been a tourist in Sydney? That's what we are today, just regular old tourists, exploring a new city."

"Okay, but is it safe for me to be out like that? What if someone recognises me? What if today's the day they plaster my face all over the news? What if the police are looking for me?"

I walk back over to her, taking both of her hands in mine. "Breathe, Emmy. You are safe. You are okay. We've looked, remember? There is no record of you being wanted by the police. There is no record of a murder, or a body being found. There is only one rogue ex-cop looking for you, Em. We will be fine. I swear I won't let him get anywhere near you."

"CAN I DRIVE?" Em asks with a huge-ass smile on her face. My heart literally palpitates. Is she serious? She wants to drive my car? I'm so fucking torn over wanting my car to remain in one piece without a fucking scratch, and giving her what she wants.

I find myself handing her the keys. There's something about the smile on her face. If I have to risk my half a million dollar Lamborghini to keep that smile there, then I will. I might cry if she destroys my car. But I'll get over it. *It's just a car. It's just a car.* I keep repeating the mantra in my head. *She is everything. This is just a car.* My fingers loosen around the keys as I place them in her palms.

"Really, you're letting me drive? Yes! Thank you, thank you, thank you." She throws her arms around my neck as she jumps up and down on the spot, full of excitement.

"Emmy, there is nothing you could ever ask me for that I'd say no to."

She raises her eyebrows at me, mischief written all over her face. "Well, there was this one thing I read about..."

"Almost nothing, babe. There are a few things I'm never saying yes to. So, whatever it is that you've read in one of your romance books, unless it involves only two people—those two people being you and me—don't even ask."

Her lips spread into a smile. "So that's a no to a threesome then?"

"That's a *fuck no,* Emily. There is no fucking chance on earth I'm ever sharing you with anyone."

Emily laughs as she makes her way to the driver's side of the car. "It's a really good thing I don't ever want you to share me then. Come on, get in. I'm about to take you on the ride of your life." She winks as she climbs into the car.

I send a little prayer up to anyone listening. *Please let my car make it out of this in one piece.* Shit, I don't think I've ever even seen Emily drive. Can she fucking drive? Getting into the passenger's side, I buckle in.

"You do have a driver's license, right?" I ask her.

"Ah, not on me. Why? Will it be a problem if we get pulled over?"

"No, but you do know how to drive? I mean, you have passed a driving test before, haven't you?" I can feel the tiny balls of sweat forming on my eyebrows. Fuck, this is making me more nervous than I anticipated.

"Relax. My daddy taught me to drive before I could even walk." She smiles.

I watch as she turns the engine. She runs her

hands over the steering wheel, then over the gear stick. "Hold on," she says.

Hold on? For what? I don't get to ask her before the tyres are screeching and she's pulling, *screaming*, up the driveway.

"Fuck, Emily Livingston, slow the fuck down!" I yell as she slams her foot on the breaks, the car coming to a stop just before the huge fucking iron gates at the front of the property—the iron gates that haven't been opened yet.

"No, fuck no. That is not how we drive this car, Emily. You are a Sunday granny driver. We ain't in some Nascar race right now. A leisurely Sunday drive is the vibe we're going for."

Emily stares at me for a minute before she speaks. When she does, her voice is low and quiet. "Josh, I don't have to drive. If you want to swap seats, we can." She actually pouts at me.

Now, I'm fucking confused. Emily has never pouted at me. That low voice she just used was different. What the fuck is wrong with her? I don't know how to handle this. Of course, I want to switch seats with her and take my damn car back. But what I want more is to see that smile back on her face. I want her to be happy and free.

"Emmy, I don't care if you want to drive. I just want you to be safe—that's all." I grab her hand and bring her fingers up to my mouth, placing a kiss on each one.

"Okay, well, as long as you're sure. I've always wanted to drive one of these fancy cars." She beams.

Why the fuck do I feel like I just got played? Did she just emotionally bribe me to get her way? I can't believe I just fell for it that easily. Damn, she's good. The goofy smile I'm now sporting is hard to hide.

"What's wrong?" Emily asks as she ever so slowly pulls out of the driveway.

"Absolutely nothing. Why would something be wrong?"

"Because you're smiling weird. Why?" She stares at my face.

"First, keep your eyes on the road. You're driving around extremely important cargo right now. Second, don't let my girlfriend hear you say I'm weird. She gets a little trigger-happy whenever she hears that." I laugh.

"Your girlfriend sounds like a cool chick. Also, I didn't say *you* were weird. I said your smile was."

"Oh, she's the coolest. Beautiful, smart, loyal, sexy, stunning… Did I mention she's beautiful?" My eyes travel up and down her body. She's wearing a royal blue sundress. It's loose-fitting with thin straps. Her hair is up in a ball of mess on top of her head, her face free of any makeup. Right now, she looks perfect.

"You've mentioned it once or twice." She smiles. "Are you ready?"

"For what?" I ask.

"For the ride of your life, baby." She laughs as she puts her foot down before shifting gears. The car takes off. I'm pulled back into my seat with the force.

Fuck me. I look ahead and see we are merging onto the freeway. Where the fuck is she even going? Why didn't I know she was such a lead foot?

I look behind us to check that the security detail is keeping up. They're not. "Ah, babe, I need you to slow down a bit. You need to let the security cars tail you. At this speed, they can't keep up."

"Why do we need security cars tailing us? And what kind of security are they if they can't keep up?"

"Because I'm a VIP, baby! And trust me, they're the best. I wouldn't put just any random security on you."

Emily looks in the rear-view mirror. With a huff, she slows down. I can at least breathe a little easier now.

CHAPTER 14

EMILY

I pull up in the almost-empty parking lot. The memories of my dad bringing me here, to this beach, hit me hard. This place holds some of my fondest memories of him. I used to hate him. My dad died saving the lives of others, and I hated him for not being able to save himself. Now, I just wish I'd told him how much I loved him.

I remember yelling at him before he left for his last tour. I remember telling him I hated him for leaving us again. That's a regret I will live with for the rest of my life. My dad was one of the best special forces soldiers this country has ever had. I'm proud to be his daughter. Although, I'm not so sure he'd be proud of me. I haven't given him anything to be proud of lately.

"You okay?" Josh asks from the passenger seat.

"Yeah, you ready to hit the beach?"

"Is there a reason you drove us an hour and a half to get to a beach? You know Bondi was only about twenty minutes from the house."

"I like this beach. It's quiet. I like that it's not crowded here. Besides, this is Soldiers Beach, you know. It's just as famous for its surf as Bondi."

I unbuckle and step out of the car. The fresh smell of the ocean assaults me, the sun warming my skin instantly. Josh walks around the car and wraps an arm around me, pulling my back against his chest. He leans his face into the crook of my neck. I tilt my head to the side, giving him better access, his lips leaving a scorching hot trail as they find their way to my ear.

"Have you been here before, Em?" His voice is husky.

"Mmm, uh, yeah. My dad used to bring me here when he was home. Come on, let's go." I remove his arm from my waist and join our fingers together. I never thought I'd like holding hands with someone as much as I like holding Josh's hand.

Walking down the million steps is exhausting, but so worth it to get to the beach below us. Once we make it to the bottom, Josh releases my hand. I look back over my shoulder at him. I can't help but drool a little at the sight before me. Josh pulls his shirt over his head and tucks it into the back of the waistband on his boardshorts.

He's standing here, in nothing but a pair of black boardshorts, all those toned, tanned muscles on display. All those delicious tattoos, for everyone to see, my name sitting proudly in the middle of his chest. I can't help but feel territorial over this man. I mean, my name is literally written on him. That means he's mine, right?

I look around the beach. There're a few people here but not anywhere near as many as what would be at Bondi. I smirk at Josh. I notice a group of young girls who are now openly staring at us, or staring at Josh anyway. I glare at them, not that they notice. Two can play that game. For the first time, in a long time, I feel comfortable in my own skin. I feel like I can be out here and people aren't going to be staring at a battered and bruised woman, my body currently free of any kind of markings. Yes, it's been a very long time since I have looked and felt this healthy.

"Hold these for me." I hand over my bag and hat to Josh.

"Sure. You know I'd carry your shit anywhere for you, babe."

"Well, that would have been useful back in high school when we had to carry around all those damn textbooks. Now, not so useful. But thanks," I say as I drag my dress over my head. I hold my hand out to Josh to return my bag.

He's standing motionless, just staring at me. Shit, I think I might have broken him this time. "Josh." I snap my fingers in front of his face. He shakes his head, coming out of whatever trance he was in.

"Emmy, where the fuck is the rest of your swimsuit?" he growls under his breath while taking my dress from me. I duck as he attempts to put it back over my head.

"This is a perfectly fine swimsuit, Josh. Don't be ridiculous. Now, are we going to stand here all day arguing over my swimmers, or are we going to get in the water?"

"Em, babe, don't get me wrong... you look fucking hot as shit. But seriously, every other guy here is checking you out. I don't know if I have it in me to refrain from cutting all of their eyes out."

I look down at my body. I'm wearing a black string bikini. It's not that skimpy, from the front at least. Josh hasn't seen the back yet.

"Don't worry, I'll keep hold of your hand so you

feel less murdery." Taking his hand, I turn and pull him towards the water, dropping my bag and kicking off my slides on the way.

"Fucking hell, I want to kill whoever the fuck designed that thing. Emmy, you know the material that's meant to cover your ass is missing. You should be asking for a refund. Fuck me, everyone's looking at your ass, babe." His hand squeezes mine tighter.

"The only person looking at my ass who even remotely matters is you. Let's not worry about what others are doing, Josh. It's just you and me."

"Okay, you and me. I like that," he says, before picking me up and running towards the water.

Once he gets waist-deep, he lets me go, dumping me into the water. My head goes under as I struggle to get my bearings. Before I can stand upright, Josh's hands drag me towards the surface. I'm coughing and spitting water everywhere. God, could I look any more awkward right now?

My hands go to my eyes, rubbing the salty residue out of them. "Oh my God, I hate you right now!" I yell as I wail in his hold.

Josh laughs and tugs me tighter against his body. Is that? It is! His hard cock is currently pressing into my stomach. How the hell is it hard right now in this cold water?

"No, you don't." He delivers his panty-dropping smirk at me.

"How on earth can you be turned on right now? I literally just spat water all over you."

"Emmy, I just have to look at you to be hard. Seeing you in this pathetic excuse of a swimsuit, all that smooth skin, feeling these curves under my palms... That's making me as hard as a fucking rock."

I wrap my legs around his waist, linking my ankles together to hold them in place. Releasing his neck, I let my body float backwards in the water, stretching my arms above my head. I love floating on the water. I love the feeling of weightlessness.

"Fuck me, Em, you're a goddamn walking pin-up." Josh growls as his hands go around my back, picking me up and pulling my chest closer to meet his.

"Well then, maybe you should pin me," I suggest.

Josh looks around the beach, then the water. "If there weren't so many people here, I would have you pinned to the sand in a heartbeat, Em."

I follow his gaze and look around. There is a good crowd of people spread out along the beach. What catches my attention is the ten men in suits standing in a line, right where I dropped my bag on the sand.

"Don't you think that's a bit of overkill, and why are they wearing suits? We're at the beach. It's odd," I voice to Josh.

"When it comes to protecting you, there is no such thing as overkill. And they're professionals; they're working. They wear suits. Trust me, Em, I'm paying them more than enough to be here." He looks over to where they stand, except one of them is now walking towards the water. Towards us.

Josh's whole body stiffens as he watches the man approach the shoreline. He waits for him to stop at the water's edge before he unclasps my legs and stands me on my feet.

"Wait here. Don't move an inch. I'll be back."

"Okay." I watch as he makes his way out of the water. And so does every other pair of female eyes on the beach. They can look all they like, but that man is mine. I'd die fighting for him if I had to.

Josh's whole body tenses as he glares at something the man shows him. He spins around and runs back towards me, making it to where I'm standing in seconds.

Taking hold of my hand, he pulls me towards the sand. "Sorry, babe, we gotta leave, now!"

"Josh, what's wrong?" I try to tug my hand free of his, which only makes him spin around and pick me up.

"Josh, stop! You're scaring me. Tell me what's going on!" I yell.

"I'll tell you once we're in the car." Josh storms up the beach, pausing at my bag. He puts me down on my feet as his security team forms a circle around us. I'm officially freaked out. Why are they all looking around, one hand each underneath their jackets, like they are waiting for the need to draw out a gun?

I can feel my body start to tremble as the panic sets in. I search Josh's face for answers, but all I can see is his anger, his eyes darkened, his jaw tensed.

"I want two cars in front, two behind. Do not let anyone get between," he directs to the men surrounding us. Picking up our belongings, he throws my bag over his shoulder before looking me up and down. Cursing under his breath, he shakes out his shirt and puts it over my head.

I absently place my arms through the sleeves. Bringing the collar up to my nose, I inhale his scent. It's somewhat soothing to my frayed nerves.

"Em, I need you to not let go of my hand right now. Stay behind me." He holds my hand tight, like I'll float away if he doesn't. I just nod my head and follow his lead.

The crowd has their phones out, filming as we make our way back to the car park surrounded by the men in suits. I'm sure they think Josh is someone famous or something. Then again, he is famous. His family is one of the wealthiest in the country; they're always in the paper.

I put my face down and let my hair curtain around me. The chances of anyone actually seeing me with all these men surrounding me are slim, but just in case, I don't want to see my face plastered on a tabloid.

JOSH WAS super quiet the whole way back into the city. I didn't have the nerve to ask him anything. I still don't know what to say. Whatever happened back on the beach has him on edge. If it scares Josh, then what the hell will it do to me?

I've never known Josh to be scared of anything; he's fearless. He was always the one causing fear in others. To see the worry in his eyes is hard for me to grasp. I want to erase his fears. I want to assure him that it will be okay. I want to slaughter whatever or whoever it was that provoked that reaction from him.

Josh parks the car at the front of the house. His fingers grip the steering wheel, turning his knuckles white. I see his mouth silently reciting each number as he counts to ten with his eyes closed. I don't move.

When he opens his eyes and pins that blue gaze on me, I finally let out the breath I didn't know I was holding in.

"Are you ready to have some fun?" he asks me, raising his eyebrows.

Talk about emotional whiplash. How the bloody hell did he just switch his emotions off like that? I'm relieved to see the fear gone—well, mostly gone. I can tell it's still there in the back of his mind, but boy, does he do a good job at faking happiness. To anyone else looking at him, you would think he didn't have a care in the world.

I know though. I can tell. "You don't have to pretend to be okay for me, Josh. Whatever happened back at the beach spooked you. I want to help. Let me help."

"Em, I promise I will tell you all about it. But right now, we have a bet to settle."

"A bet? What bet?"

"You don't remember? Last night, you made a bet with Bray that you were a better shot than him."

"I don't remember doing that. Why would I do that? Hold up… what exactly did I bet?" I ask, panicked. I don't exactly have anything to gamble with.

"Uh, I may have placed a small wager on it." He averts his eyes, looking out the windshield of the car.

"How small, Josh?"

"The details are fuzzy, but from what I recall, it was around two."

"Two thousand dollars? Josh, you cannot bet two thousand dollars on me. That's insane." My voice rises with panic. What if I lose? What if he didn't bet on me to win, and I actually do win?

"Don't be ridiculous, Emmy. I didn't bet two thousand. It was two mil."

My mouth falls open and shut. "Holy bloody shit! Joshua McKinley, no! Just NO! We need a goddamn intervention up in here, because that has to be the stupidest thing I've ever seen you do. And that's saying a lot, because you once hit our math teacher and got yourself a month's worth of after school detention. *On purpose.*"

"I got to spend a week in the detention hall staring at you. It was worth it."

"Do you even remember why I was in detention, Josh?"

"No, all I remember is hearing you being given a week of detentions. I knew I was going to be in that hall with you. Do you know the kind of riffraff who frequented the detention hall?"

"You?"

"Well, yeah, but also, all those other jerks. If I

hadn't been there, trust me, Em, you would have been in for a week of hell."

I screw my face up. Does he think it wasn't a week of hell having his intense gaze on me? My skin prickling for the whole hour we sat there silently? I'd never been hornier in my life. The things I'd imagine Josh doing to me then… I would snap out of my daydream to see the smirk on his face. He knew what I was thinking about—*the ass*.

"I don't know. I remember spending the week daydreaming and fantasising about a boy. It was hours well spent. I barely even noticed anyone else in the room. But just so we're clear, it was your fault I got detention that day."

"Em, you were daydreaming about *me*. Don't even try to pretend you weren't. And how was it my fault?"

"Maybe I was. Maybe I wasn't. It was your fault because there was a note left at my desk. A note addressed to Emmy. I was so frustrated I didn't know where these notes were bloody coming from that I screamed."

"How is that my fault?"

"Come on, Josh, you are the only person to ever call me Emmy. You and I both know you were writing those notes."

"Maybe I was. Maybe I wasn't. Come on, let's get

in and show Bray why you don't fuck with Emmy McKinley."

"Livingston. I'm not a McKinley, Josh."

"If I say it enough, it will eventuate. And trust me, Em, you will be a McKinley."

CHAPTER 15

JOSH

Emily stops me before we're about to walk through the front door. "Josh, did you bet on me to lose? Because I can purposely lose if you need me to."

"Fuck no, I didn't bet on you to lose. Em, I bet on you to win. Although, I don't really care if you win or lose. It's just a bit of fun, Emmy. Relax."

"Two million dollars is not a bit of fun, Joshua."

"We make that in a day. It's fine. You *have* shot a gun before, right? Do you need a quick rundown on what to do?" I'm not sure why I expect her to have range experience. She's just always been the girl who can conquer anything she attempts.

She smiles at me. *A mischievous smile.* "I guess we're about to find out."

When we walk down to the basement, where my father had an indoor gun range built, we find everyone waiting. Bray is jumping up and down like a damn lunatic.

"What the fuck is wrong with you?" I ask.

"Just warming up the muscles. Where the fuck are your clothes?" He bounces around, punching the air.

"Who needs clothes when you look like this?" I ask, waving a hand down my bare chest. I probably should have taken Em to get dressed before we came in here; she doesn't seem to mind though.

"You know you're not getting into the ring, moron. You're shooting a fucking handgun." Looking at Emily, I whisper in her ear, "You are at least a thousand times smarter than him, babe. You've got this."

"This is going to be fun." She laughs.

"Okay, let's get this show on the road. Hope you got your bank on standby, McKinley. Sorry, Emily, nothing personal, but you're about to get beat," Bray says, still jumping around like a fool.

"Well, that's okay. It's about having fun, right? Not winning or losing," Emily replies in a sugary-sweet voice. A tone I haven't heard since high school.

I laugh. Whatever she's got up her sleeve, it's going to be good.

"That's what all the losers say." Bray laughs.

I watch as Emily walks off to the side of the room, and to the table that hosts a spread of handguns. She looks at all the choices, biting her lip. Fuck, she seems nervous and unsure. Maybe I overestimated her comfort level...

"Okay, you go first. Show me how it's done, Bray," Emily says quietly.

I pull her into my arms and whisper in her ear, "Em, you know you don't have to do this, right? Just say so, and we'll get out of here."

"I want to do this. Follow my lead, okay?"

"Well, that's easy. I'd follow you anywhere, babe."

Her smile eases my mind. She's okay; she can handle this.

"Bray, calm the hell down before you shoot someone!" Ella shouts.

"Don't worry, El, if he shoots you, I'll make sure he ends up pig food." I wink at her.

"My hero..." Ella pretends to swoon.

"Ella, what the fuck? You are not giving my *favourite brother* title to him." Bray points to me.

"I'm pretty sure you've never actually had that title. Has he, El?" Zac grunts from his perch on the couch.

"You know what? I don't have a favourite brother. I hate you all equally."

"Ouch, what'd I do?" I ask, pretending to be wounded.

"You orchestrated this whole charade. You knew Bray wouldn't turn down a bet. You're a sore loser, Josh. How are you going to cope if he wins and Emily loses?"

"Emily never loses," I say confidently. Emily coughs behind me.

"Ah, Josh, that's not true. Debate team, year eleven. I lost."

"Well, yeah, but you went up against me, babe. Of course, you wouldn't stand a chance against me."

Emily tilts her head. "Okay, well, how about after I beat Bray, you try to beat me at target practice?"

Her tone is way too confident. She must know how to shoot. "What are the stakes?" I ask her.

She leans up and whispers so only I can hear her, "If you win, I'll be your sex slave. I'll let you have any part of me you want."

Her cheeks redden as she looks me in the eye, winking. I swallow, because damn, do I want every inch of her. There's one part I haven't had yet, and I'm itching to claim it as mine. "And if you win?"

"Mmm, if I win, I want the papers to the Lambo." She laughs.

"My car?" I ask, appalled. She did not just ask me to bet my fucking car…

"Are you scared you'll lose, Josh?"

"No, I'm scared you'll win," I reply.

"That's the same as you losing." Ella laughs.

"As long as I've got Emmy, I'm always winning. It's a deal. Now, let's get on with it. I want to claim my prize." I wink at Emily. She swallows, a little unsure.

"Don't worry, babe, I'll make sure I lube up your little puckered hole real good before I make it mine," I whisper in her ear. She lets out a quiet moan before she composes herself, turning away from me with pink cheeks.

"Okay, everyone, muffs on. Bray, I swear to God if you shoot someone, I'll bury you myself," Zac says, handing me two sets of ear protection.

"Where's your wife?" I ask him as I take the equipment.

His body stiffens at my question. "Why?"

"She makes you so much more bearable to be around. You should make sure she's with you everywhere you go. I think you'd find you'd have more friends than just my brother."

"Really? How many friends have you got, Josh? Last I heard, that count was still zero, you know, 'cause everyone's too worried you'll turn them to pig food when you go off on a crazy tangent."

Without thinking, I step in front of Emily and peel her fingers from the firearm she's currently holding. Given the death stare she's delivering Zac right now, I'm not sure she wouldn't actually shoot him.

"I'm just gonna hold this for you, babe," I say, removing the gun from her tense palms.

"Can't I just shoot him once, Josh? I'll make sure it's... like... in a knee or something. Nothing lethal," Emily seethes.

"Trust me, babe, I've had the same thought... *more than once*." I glance over at Zac's unimpressed face, though he does side-eye Emily as if he's a little worried. He should be.

"Emily, I'm sorry. I'll try to remember to keep my thoughts about your boyfriend to myself a little better."

"You should look in the mirror, Zac. Those who throw stones... You know, glass houses and all."

"Okay, if you all don't shut the fuck up and put those muffs on, I'm starting anyway. I'm sure Richie Rich over there can afford the hearing aids you will all need," Bray calls out as he takes a stance at the firing line, his barrel aimed at the target.

"It's okay. I don't need you to stand up for me,

Em. I'm a big boy. I can take whatever any of these pricks have to say," I tell her, securing her ear protection in place.

Bray finishes his turn, dragging the target inwards across the lane. I can see he didn't do too badly, all rounds striking the upper body.

"Your turn, Emily. Good luck beating that." He smiles, proud of himself. I actually don't know if she can beat it. He's a good shot.

Emily looks over the range of handguns. She picks up a few, hefting them in her hands and feeling the weight of each. She doesn't look satisfied with the choices.

"Josh, is this the only arsenal you have?" she asks.

"Are you expecting a whole armoury, Em?"

"Well, yeah, kind of." She shrugs.

I unlock a door that leads to an actual armoury. Our father liked guns. I've never really been too keen on them, but for some reason, Dean has kept them all here.

"Holy shit!" Emily walks into the room, her eyes wide. She heads straight for the three sniper rifles sitting along the back wall.

Her fingers lightly run over one of the stocks, and a distant look crosses her features.

"Em, you okay?"

"Ah, yeah. I'm good. I don't need these. I'm just

going to pick a little handgun." She walks around me and out of the secured space. I follow close behind. Whatever just went through her mind made her sad. I can't fucking stand seeing that despondent look in her eyes. It breaks me every single time.

I watch silently as Emily picks up a handgun. She doesn't even really look at it. Instead, she walks up to the line, aims and shoots. One shot. Turning around, she says to Bray, "Bring it in. I believe you owe Josh a fair sum of cash."

He tugs the line forward. The whole room is speechless as we look at the shot she just made. One clean round, dead centre through the forehead of the printed silhouette.

"What the actual fuck? Of course you'd find yourself a little assassin!" Bray shouts.

"Pay up, Williamson." I smirk at him.

"Fine, but I was duped. You're like the target shooting version of a pool shark. Where the fuck did you learn to shoot like that, anyway?" Bray stares at Emily, waiting for an answer.

"Don't be a sore loser. Sorry, guys, Emily and I have plans." I bend down and throw her over my shoulder.

"Josh, we haven't had our turn. I want to win that bloody car, damn it. Put me down!" she yells as we exit the room.

"You can have the car, Em. I'll buy another one." I take the stairs two at a time. I need to get back up to my room. We make it to the hallway, but deciding I can't wait another minute, I walk into the first room I see and slam the door shut. We're in the library. This will work.

Laying Emily down on the large mahogany desk, I lift my shirt, which she's been wearing since the beach, over her head and toss it aside. She's left in that tiny fucking bikini. Pulling on all the strings, I remove the scraps of material from her body. She's like an angel laid out before me. A feast fit for a king.

"I'd love to take my time and worship this piece of art you call a body, but I need to be buried inside you now," I growl.

Emily moans and spreads her legs apart. It's like a huge welcome home banner for my cock. I undo my boardshorts and kick them off, stroking my cock a few times as I stare down at Emily's weeping pussy.

"Are you ready for me, Emmy? Are you ready for me to fuck you into oblivion?" I ask as I line myself up with her entrance.

"Yes, Josh, hurry up already."

I slam into her as soon as I hear the word *yes*. That's all I need, her consent for me to let the beast inside me unleash.

I stay still for a few minutes while I'm buried to

the hilt in her warm channel. I could die a happy man right now and still feel like my life was complete.

Once I feel her hips start to move, I know she's had time to adjust to my intrusion. I don't start off slow. I don't hold back. I give her everything I've got. I told her I was going to fuck her into oblivion, and that's exactly what I plan to do.

I'm going hard, her screams filling the room along with the sound of our bodies smashing together. I need more. I always need more.

Pulling out, I flip her over so she's lying flat on her stomach, her plump ass on display. My fingers slide down the crack, twirling around the outside edges of her little puckered hole.

"This ass is mine, Emmy." Her body stiffens. She's not ready for that, but she will be.

I slowly guide myself into her wet, warm piece of heaven. Once I'm buried all the way, I tell her, "Hold on, Em, this is going to be fast and rough."

She obeys without question. Her arms go out to the side of the desk as her hands fold over the ledge.

I pump in and out of her. I can feel her walls contracting. I know she's so fucking close, and so am I. Bringing my thumb down to her clit, I circle around while my other thumb goes straight to that forbidden hole. As soon as my digit pushes through the tight ring, Emmy loses it. She screams out my name as well as a bunch of other incoherent words. But it's *my* name that she screams loudest. Anyone walking by would know exactly who's fucking her. Who's made her feel this fucking good. Who's claimed her.

Her walls choke my cock, quivering as I drive into her a few more times before roaring with my own release. I collapse over her, catching my weight with my hands so she isn't forced to bear it.

On shaky legs, I reach for a tissue box and clean her up. Turning her over, I sit her upright and put the shirt back over her head before adjusting my shorts.

"I fucking love you, Emily, so damn much," I whisper into her hairline as I kiss her forehead.

"I know the feeling," she replies.

"Care to tell me where the hell you learnt to shoot with such accuracy?"

"My dad was a special forces sniper, Josh. Who do you think I learnt from?" She raises her eyebrows.

"Your dad taught you how to shoot, Emily? You were fifteen when he died. You shouldn't have even been near guns."

"Calm your farm. I learnt to shoot when I was

five. My dad said it was in our blood. I always had good aim," she says proudly.

"Well, you're now two million dollars richer. Thanks to your little sharking ways." I laugh.

"I don't want his money. Tell him to keep it, Josh. I don't need it."

"No, you don't, but it's a lesson for him not to be such a smartass all the damn time. Don't worry, he can afford it, babe. Come on, let's go shower the salt and sand off."

CHAPTER 16

EMILY

Josh has cooked breakfast again. I have a full plate of bacon, eggs, hash browns and toast. I'm starting to think he doesn't trust me to cook for him. But damn, this bacon is good. I can't get enough of it right now.

"You do know I can cook, right? Maybe I should cook you breakfast one day," I say around a mouthful of crispy bacon. Josh laughs and places another couple of pieces of bacon on my plate.

"Em, you don't need to cook. I like doing things for you."

"I'm going to get fat if you keep feeding me like

this. You won't be so keen on me when I'm the size of this house," I point out.

"You could be the size of an elephant and I'd still fuck you just as much as I do now. I will love you no matter what you look like, babe."

"Charming. But I think I'd like to cook for you. How about dinner? Tonight? What's your favourite meal?" My eyebrows draw down at the realisation I don't know what his favourite meal is. I should know something so simple. He seems to know everything about me… sometimes before I even do.

"Emmy, it's okay. We are going to have the rest of our lives for you to be barefoot and pregnant in our kitchen. But if you insist on cooking me dinner, I like steak." I almost choke on the bacon. I cough it up and it comes spitting out onto the bench.

"You-you want me to be p-pregnant?" I finally manage to get out.

"Well, I'm not opposed to the idea, but if you don't want kids, Emmy, it's okay too. We'll get an alpaca."

"I-I don't know." Shit, is it getting hotter in here? I can't breathe. I pull at the collar of my top, moving it away from my throat. Looking around the room, I eye the door that leads to the outside. I can make it there. If I run really fast, I can make it to that door.

Just as I'm about to get up, Josh's arms hug me

tight to his chest. "Emmy, it's okay. You're okay. I'm right here. You are safe. Just breathe, Em." He rocks me as he smooths his hand down my hair and whispers me promises that I know aren't entirely true.

I'm not okay. I'm probably never going to be okay again. This is never going to stop. I thought I was finally starting to be better. This hasn't happened for a while. But now, the mention of being pregnant has pushed me over the edge. The memory of the time I was so happy to find myself pregnant is vividly playing like a movie in my mind.

I wait the three minutes the box says it takes for the stick to show the results. Nervousness and excitement run through me as I sit here. It's going to be okay. Whatever it says, it will be okay. Trent will be happy with a baby. Who doesn't love babies?

Turning the stick over, my heart explodes with an unexpected feeling. I can't pinpoint what it is, but I know it's a good one. Two lines are visible on the display pad. Pregnant, I'm pregnant. I'm going to be someone's mother.

I shake the thoughts from my mind. I cannot go back there. I won't be that person again. The mother who was too weak to save her own unborn child from the hell her husband inflicted on her. I won't do it.

"Emmy, what the fuck happened? You've been

pregnant?" Josh keeps his voice soft, calm, even with his colourful choice of language.

I shake my head. "I-I can't..." I try to lie. I try to tell him no, but the words won't come out.

"It's okay. You don't have to tell me right now."

My whole body relaxes in his arms.

"Em, if you were to get knocked up, you know I'd take care of you, right? I'd make sure you had the best doctors. Your child would want for nothing."

"My child? Josh, if I got knocked up, as you so eloquently call it, it would be your child too. I don't see anyone else painting my walls with their seed around here, do you?" I'm not sure why I'm so riled up all of a sudden. It's not like we haven't had this conversation before...

"No one around here would be stupid enough to even try to get near your walls, Emmy. And yes, it would be my child, but I pray that our children have more of you than me in them. The world could use more angels like you." He kisses my lips gently. I pull him down to deepen the kiss.

"Don't mind me, kids." Sam's voice tears us apart. I glare at him. How dare he interrupt when I finally manage to find my happy place again. I'm aware that this co-dependency Josh and I have going on is anything but healthy. I just don't care enough to do anything about it.

Sam laughs at my icy glare. "Emily, you've been around him too long. That stare is almost a perfect match for his."

"Careful, mate, it's the quiet ones you have to watch out for," Dean says as he digs into the fridge.

"Why are you here, Sam? It's fucking Saturday," Josh grunts, ignoring Dean's comment.

"Ah, I need that fancy signature of yours on some documents for the Casey merger."

I've heard that before. I'd bet there is no bloody Casey merger, and it's some sort of boy's code for: *I've got shit to tell you, but not in front of others.*

"I'll meet you in the library in five," Josh says.

"Hey, Josh, how long exactly does a merger with another company usually take?" I ask.

"It depends on a lot of influencing factors. You want to come be my COO, Em?"

"No, I was just curious. But whatever Sam has to tell you, I want to hear it too."

Josh shakes his head. "You are too damn smart for your own good sometimes. I promise I will tell you whatever you want to know. Are you going to finish your breakfast?"

I nod my head, because, well, bacon. I'm not about to let it go to waste.

"Dean, have breakfast with Emily for me. I won't

be long." Josh throws the order out as he exits the room.

Dean's eyebrows go up to his hairline. "Why me?" he asks to the ceiling, before looking directly at me and pointing. "*You,* do not move a muscle, not even a hair. If I return you with so much as a hair out of place, he'll know, and I'll be pig food."

I don't know how to take Dean. Is he joking? He looks serious. I'm not sure why, but I've always gotten this impression that he didn't like me very much. I've never really even had a one-on-one conversation with him. I guess now's my chance to find out why he doesn't like me.

"You don't like me very much, do you?" I blurt out. Dean looks taken aback by my question; he just stares at me contemplatively.

"Why would you think that? I like you just fine," he finally answers.

"No, you don't. Why not?" I can't help the fact that the people pleaser in me wants to come out and fix his impression of me.

"It's not that I don't like you… It's not you at all. It's Josh. You didn't see the mess he was after you left, Emily. For almost two years, I had to pick his drunk ass up off the floor every damn day. He tried just about every drug he could, in order to make not having you more bearable. I'd wake up, night after night, to him screaming out your name in his sleep. So, it's not that I don't like *you*. It's that I don't like the power you hold over my brother. You are the only person on earth who has the power to destroy him. I don't want to see him go down that road of despair ever again."

I'm speechless. How do I even respond to that? I don't even notice that I'm crying until Dean hands me a tissue. "For the love of God, don't tell him I made you cry."

"I won't. But just so you know, I didn't leave him. He told me to leave. He didn't want me here. It wasn't exactly a piece of cake for me either." I get up, suddenly angry that Josh did this to us. Why didn't he come after me? If he was so broken up over not having me, why didn't he just come and find me?

I know he had his reasons for keeping me away, but I'm still filled with irrational anger. I'm angry at him. I'm angry at the situation I've now put us in. And I'm angry at everyone trying to keep us apart. Are we ever going to get our happily ever after? Because I'm more than ready for it. I want it *yesterday*.

I storm towards the library. "Wait! Where are you going?" Dean calls out.

"To slap some sense into your idiot brother," I retort.

"Shit, Emily, wait up. You should just wait for Josh to finish his meeting. Then, I'll hold him down while you slap that sense into him," Dean offers.

I'm not deterred by his attempts to stop me. The force I push the library door open with has it slamming against the wall. When I step into the room, Josh and Sam have guns pointed in my direction. I freeze. I swear they think they're playing an adult-sized game of cops and robbers sometimes.

"Fuck, Emmy," Josh hisses as he lowers his sidearm. "What's wrong?" He looks behind me to Dean, who has just caught up with me.

"Ah, I tried to stop her," Dean says.

Josh pauses in front of me, bringing his palms up to cup my cheeks. I swipe his hands away from my face. He grits his teeth as he puts his arms down. "Em, babe, what's wrong?"

I look behind him to see Sam scrambling to pack up a heap of papers they have spread out on the desk. I look up to Josh briefly. There's confusion and hurt in his eyes. But I need to know what it is they're trying to hide from me.

I walk around Josh and pull the stack of papers out of Sam's hands. He was too stunned by my actions to put up much of a fight. The moment I drop the papers to the desk and fan them out, I wish they had stopped me. This isn't something I can ever unsee.

Spread out in front of me is a heap of photos. Photos of girls' bodies. Photos of me... from when I was with Trent. Photos of my broken and bruised body. "W-w-why do you have these?" I ask directly to Josh. Why would they be looking at these?

I step away from the desk, and Josh's face falls. "Emmy, it's not. It's..." Running his fingers roughly through his hair, he curses. He makes his way towards me, stopping only when he sees me retreat further away from him.

"Emily, this is the work of Detective Jones. He..." Sam's cut off by Josh.

"Get the fuck out of here. Now! Leave!"

I've never heard Josh sound so animalistic. I watch as Sam and Dean both look towards me, unsure whether they should leave me here or not. I nod my head. I'm okay. Josh won't hurt me. I'm not scared *of* him... I'm scared *for* him.

I need to help him. I don't like seeing him so lost. As soon as Dean shuts the door behind him, I walk over to Josh and pull his hands down from where they are currently pulling at his hair.

He looks at me, but his gaze is more vacant than I've ever seen. "Josh?" I don't know what to say to him right now. I should know how to help him.

"Emmy, you shouldn't have seen them. You weren't meant to see them. I should be protecting you from all of this."

I pull him over to the couch and push him down. Climbing on top of him, I hold his face in my hands, so he has to look at me.

"This is not your fault, Josh. You *are* protecting me. Where do you think I would be right now if you never found me?"

"I should have protected you from *that* ever happening. You didn't deserve to endure that... You should never have been there." Josh wraps his arms around my back, pulling my body against his.

"Nobody deserves to live what I went through. But I survived. I'm still here. I know I don't always handle things great... I know I have issues. But I need you to tell me what's going on. I can't be kept in the dark, Josh."

"It's not a burden I want you to carry, Emmy."

"We don't lie to each other, remember? We don't keep secrets. It's you and me, against the world, Josh."

He stares at me without saying a word for what seems like hours, but in actuality, is probably only minutes. Looking over the pile of papers on the desk, he shakes his head no. He doesn't want to tell me.

"The pictures came from a warehouse Sam and I went to the other day. We had a lead on where Jones was hiding out. When we got there, all that we saw were three bodies and a wall of photos. A whole wall… covered in photos of you."

"How would he get those pictures? Some of them are from years ago."

"I don't know. That's not all. Jones has been sending emails. Every day. Graphic messages of what he wants to do to you when he finds you."

"Why didn't you tell me?"

"I don't want you to worry. I'm going to find this arsehole, Em. I will make sure he never gets his hands on you."

"I wish I knew what he wanted with me. I don't recall ever meeting him. I don't remember Trent ever mentioning anyone by that name. Maybe Trent's brother would know something. What if I called him?"

"I don't think he knows anything, Em. I've had guys following him for the past few weeks. He lives a mundane life with his wife and kids. Goes to work, goes home, takes his kids to soccer on weekends."

"I only met him a few times during the first year I dated Trent. After that, I never saw him again. It's worth a try, right? We know there is no real warrant for me. Somebody went to great efforts to cover up

Trent's death, to make it look like he left town. I'm not a suspect, right?"

"Em, there's something else Sam just found. That whole marriage paperwork you signed... it was fake. You were never legally married."

"I wasn't...? So, hypothetically, if I wanted to get married today, I could?" I ask him. Visions of running off and marrying Josh play on repeat in my mind. Would he want to marry me? I know he's mentioned it before... but is he serious? Could I just ask him, instead of waiting for him to pop the question?

CHAPTER 17

JOSH

My mind is all over the place. The hurt look on Emily's face when she saw the pictures we had of her haunts me. I'm not entirely sure I trust my own brain at the moment, because I swear she asked if she could get married today.

I stare at her face. She looks determined. Fuck, maybe she did just ask to get married.

"Em, is that your way of asking me to marry you? Because if it is, the answer is fuck yes!"

The smile that spreads across her face lightens my heart; it eases the tension in my body. "Josh, will you marry me? Today?" she asks.

"Emily Livingston, you know I'd marry you any day that ends in Y. *But* you deserve a wedding. A proper, fancy-as-shit ceremony. The big white dress, the flowers, all of that shit little girls dream of having. I don't want you to settle for anything less than you deserve."

"I don't need any of that, Josh. All I need is you. All I want is you. *Forever*. But it's okay. I get that someone in your position can't just run off and get married. I can wait." She averts her eyes.

Tilting her chin, so she's looking back up at me, I ask, "What do you mean someone in my position?"

"Well, I don't know if you noticed, but you're a McKinley, Josh. And not just any McKinley. You are the CEO of McKinley Industries. Obviously, you can't marry someone on a whim. You need to take precautions. You need to organise a prenup, which I will happily sign, FYI."

Shifting slightly, I reach for my phone in my pocket and scroll through until I find the number I need. "Hold that thought, Em. And, FYI, we don't need a prenup. Your ass is crazy if you think I'd ever let you divorce me."

I press the number and dial, before placing the call on speaker so Emily can hear. It rings a few times before he picks up.

"McKinley, is there a good reason you're calling me on a Saturday morning?" he groans.

"Judge Thomas, I'm calling in a favour." I smile at Em, who is sitting as still as a damn statue, waiting to see what I'm doing.

"Josh, if you're in the lockup, call your brother to bail you out," the judge replies.

"I don't need bailing out. I need to get married. Today. I need you to do whatever it is you have to do to make it legal. *Today*." Emily's eyes go wide.

"Ah, Josh, are you being blackmailed? Gun to your head? Or just insane? Don't tell me you knocked up some bird and need to make it official before anyone finds out?"

"No. How long do you need? To have all the paperwork together? To get this done?"

"Ah, I'll have it done by six tonight, my office. If you're late, I won't be waiting around. I'm going to need the details of the poor woman you've convinced to marry you."

"We'll be there. I'll have Sam send you everything you need."

Hanging up the phone, I pull Emily's face into mine, melding my lips with hers. My tongue seeks entrance into her mouth, which she eagerly grants. She grinds down on my cock as she moans against my lips, tugging on my hair. I let her take everything she wants for a few minutes before I lose it and regain control.

Flipping her over and laying her back on the couch, I settle myself between her legs. "Mmm, maybe we should refrain, you know, until after we're married," I mumble into the crook of her neck as my fingers work their way into her panties, circling her little nub.

"You can stop if you want. I'll just go and finish myself off. *Alone*," she growls.

I laugh. "Emmy, this pussy is mine. Your pleasure, it's mine. Mine to give you. Mine to revel in. You are mine." I bite down softly on her shoulder as I insert two fingers inside her.

"Well, your pussy wants to be brought to a quivering mess, Josh. Make it happen."

Holy shit, she's demanding when she's horny. I fucking love how she comes right out of her shell in these moments.

"Say *please* and I just might, Emmy." My fingers pump slowly in and out of her, while I use my weight to hold down her hips, stopping her from being able to chase the tempo she desires.

Emily glares at me, her mouth clamped shut. She doesn't want to say please. Her hips fight my hold, trying to grind into my hand harder. I keep my strokes slow, teasing, my thumb lightly grazing her clit. I know I'm driving her out of her mind. She's so fucking turned on right now her juices are dripping down my hand.

Looking at my left hand, as it pumps in and out of her, I have a vision of this same moment, except with a gold band on my finger. "I can't wait until your sweet juices are running all over my wedding band. Tonight, when you're officially my wife, we're doing this again."

"Josh, you won't live to see tonight if you don't give me what I want, now." Emily's face scrunches.

I chuckle into her shoulder. "But I love having you squirming, wanting, beneath me."

"Please, Josh, I can't take it anymore." She gasps as I increase the thrusts of my fingers, grinding my thumb down hard on her clit as soon as that 'please' left her mouth.

"Oh God, don't stop, yes!" she screams as her core begins to spasm within seconds. Her inner muscles tighten around my fingers, squeezing them almost to the point of pain.

Removing my fingers, I bring them to my mouth and suck them clean, one at a time. Emily's body shivers beneath me while she watches. As soon as I've finished, she pulls my face down to hers. Her tongue swirls around my own. Moaning into my mouth, she groans as I line my cock up with her entrance.

I break our kiss, about to seek her permission, when she tilts her hips up, drawing my cock into her pussy.

"Arghh, fuck, you're so goddamn fucking perfect, Emmy. I never want to go a day without being buried inside you."

"Well, you should probably put a ring on it then." She laughs.

"Six o'clock tonight, babe, my ring will be on this dainty little finger of yours. My name will be yours. Everything I have will be yours," I promise her.

"I just want you. Just give me you," she whispers breathlessly as I start to slowly move.

"You've always had me, Emmy. I'll be yours forever and more."

"WHAT DO you mean you're getting married tonight?" Sam asks, downing the shot of whisky, which it's still way too fucking early to be drinking.

"Exactly that. Six tonight. Judge Thomas's office. If you don't want to be there, you don't have to be. I won't lose any sleep if you're not."

"Of course, I'll fucking be there. I'm just having a

hard time believing she agreed to marrying you. Should I get her a shrink? I mean, you are both as fucking cr…" Sam cuts himself off and looks around the empty room before continuing in a whisper, "crazy as each other."

The look of utter terror on his face as he whispered the singular word is hilarious. It's hard to think that a six-foot-something man is scared of little ol' Emmy. Don't get me wrong, I won't ever be underestimating her when she's holding a gun ever fucking again. I can't believe I didn't know she was a little sniper.

"It was her idea. She asked me," I say proudly. There was no begging on my part, although I was fully prepared to beg when I did get around to asking her. I wanted to give her the fairy-tale proposal. What is she going to tell our grandchildren when they ask about the details of her engagement, or what her wedding was like?

Fuck, can I go through with this rushed elopement, knowing I'm ripping her off when it comes to memories? Unless, I give her the memories. I can do that. I already have a ring. I've had it for a few weeks, waiting for the right moment to give it to her. No better time than the present, right?

"I've gotta go do something. Email me the place

you found. I'll go check it out later," I tell Sam, before exiting the room.

"Do not go alone, Josh," he yells after me.

I don't bother answering him. He and I both know if I want to go alone, I fucking will. He's pinged Jones's IP address (from today's grotesque email) to a new location. I fully intend to go and check it out. First, though, I need to give Emily the proposal she deserves.

I find Emily in our bedroom. I head straight for the wardrobe, where there is a little safe currently housing her engagement ring. Retrieving the ring, I walk out to her and take her Kindle from her hands; she glares at me while her fingers white-knuckle grip the device.

"Relax, Emmy, I'm just putting it down over here," I say as I tug harder and place the e-reader on the other side of the bed.

"Come dance with me," I say, holding out my hand, waiting for her.

"Dance? You want to dance? In here? There's no music, Josh," she says while taking my hand and standing up, despite her protest.

"Well, I can fix that. Hold on." I pull out my phone and flick through a Spotify playlist I have, which I've filled with songs that remind me of her, finding the perfect song for this moment.

"I Get to Love You" by Ruelle plays softly while I take her in my arms. The words resonate with me. Loving Emily is the best thing I will ever do in my lifetime. It's the only thing I've ever done with my complete heart and soul invested in the outcome.

"Emily, I don't know what I ever did to get you. But whatever mistake God made when he gave me you, it's too late now. I'm keeping you. There're no takebacks happening here." Leaning into her, I inhale her scent, gently kissing her forehead before continuing. I try to swallow the emotions so I can get everything out that I need to tell her.

"I love you more than I've ever loved anything in my entire life. I know that I'm a lot to take at times. I know I'm far from being even remotely deserving of your love. But I promise I will try every day to be a better man, a man worthy of your time. I will do whatever I have to do to ensure that you know just how loved you are. I will cherish you. I will honour you. I will fucking worship you every day for the rest of my life."

Letting go of her, I take the ring out of my pocket and hold it up to her finger. "Emily Livingston, will you do me the honour of becoming my wife, my partner in life, my queen?"

I wait for her response before I slide the ring onto her finger. Her eyes water as she brings her other hand up to her mouth. "Yes, however, I'm pissed you outdid my crappy little attempt at a proposal."

I laugh. "Em, you proposing to me is the best thing that's ever happened to me. I want you to have the kind of stories you can tell our grandchildren about. I don't want to rip away the memories you should have."

"I don't need the memories as long as I have you, Josh."

This girl is fucking everything. I know heads are rolling up in heaven at the fuck up someone made by pairing her with me. I smile because, in this case, the devil really has won.

"OKAY, you are going to be at the courthouse, right? You're not going to stand me up, are you?" Emily asks me as I'm about to leave.

"Emmy, I'd never fucking stand you up. I can't wait for you to be Mrs. McKinley. I'll meet you there at 6:00 p.m. *Sharp*. Don't be late," I tell her, kissing her already kiss-swollen lips.

"I don't understand why we can't go together. We've already done every other unspeakable thing together, Josh. It's not exactly going to be bad luck."

"I just have an errand I need to run first. Besides, it's a memory you can share with the grandkids—how you got ready with Ella and met me at the courthouse. You'll tell them how your breath was taken away by how stunning I looked in a tux. That your heart pitter-pattered the moment you got to put that ring on my finger and locked my ass down forever." I give her my best panty-melting smirk, hoping to ease some of her worries just a little.

"I'll tell them all of that and so much more. I love you, Josh. And, in case I forget to tell you later, thank you for choosing me."

"I will always choose you, Emmy."

As I'm walking out of the house, a sense of unease settles in me. It's not prewedding jitters. I have no doubt that Emily is my one. I've never doubted that. But something else is off. I just don't know what it is.

I read the address that Sam sent me earlier. He said he had a couple of guys scoping the place out, but they hadn't found anything yet. If there's even a scrap of information that will lead me to this fucker, then I want it found, which means I'm going to go there and search for myself.

I have three hours before I have to meet Emily. I figure I can check this place out, change in the car and then head to the courthouse.

Pulling up to the deserted house, I'm pretty sure I'm not going to find jack shit here. The place looks like it's been empty for decades. An old fibro cottage, surrounded by overgrown grass and weeds. I double-check that I've got the right address. Looking around the street, I don't see another goddamn car. I thought Sam said he had a few guys staking out the place.

I'll be in and out. I'm going to be fucking pissed if I walk into a goddamn spider web in this mess. Slamming the car door, I stomp towards the front of the house. The door is already slightly ajar. Pushing it open further, I look down the empty entranceway.

The floorboards creak as I walk through the back of the house. Just as I suspected, there is nothing here. Not a sign of life, or of anyone having ever been here. Deciding I'm wasting my time, I turn and head back for the entrance.

I'm halfway down the hall when I hear the footsteps behind me. Turning around, I see him, Jones, right before a sharp pain radiates through my head and my vision blurs. Dizzy and disorientated, I grab onto the wall to hold myself, then there's another sharp jolt to my head and my knees hit the floor.

CHAPTER 18

EMILY

"Are you nervous? It's okay if you are. I'd offer to help you escape if you wanted to run now, but I don't have a death wish." Ella laughs.

"Josh would never hurt you. He loves you. I'm not nervous. Should I be nervous? I don't know why, but I'm not. I just feel like I've been waiting a really long time for this moment. I wish I could share it with my mum. I wish my dad were still alive to give me away, but I'm not nervous."

"Do you think your dad would have approved of Josh?" Ella asks, smiling around her champagne glass.

"Ah, no. Definitely not. But he would have come

around eventually. He would have seen how much Josh loves me, and that's all that would matter to him. Are you sure this isn't too much? I mean, we're just going to the courthouse."

I stare at my reflection as my hands skim down the floor-length, white silk dress Ella brought up to me. It's beautiful. The dress has a low back, the material dipping almost all the way down to the top of my ass. The halter bodice ties around the back of my neck, leaving two long white ribbons dangling along my spine.

It's low cut at the front, like really freaking low cut. There's a slit right down the middle of the dress, which goes to my belly button. Ella had to put some sort of sticky tape on the dress to keep it in place.

She's been a godsend the last few hours, helping me get ready. She's done my hair in some weird kind of updo with a heap of twists and curls. I couldn't recreate it even if I tried. I instructed her to keep the makeup light, simple and natural. So, with a neutral nude lip colour and a bit of dark mascara, I'm pretty much ready to go.

"I'm under strict orders to make sure you have a dress that you'll be able to tell your grandkids about. And this dress is exactly that. Josh was rambling something about memories. I tuned out after I heard the words *white dress*."

I can't help but smile at Josh's insistence that we create memories together we can tell our grandkids about. I'm still not one hundred percent sold on the idea of kids, but the memories, I'm more than sold on having those to treasure for all time.

"Emily, hurry your ass up. I'm not getting shot because I didn't get you there on time," Sam hollers from behind the closed bedroom door.

Ella walks to the door, opening it to an annoyed-looking Sam. He glances over his shoulder at me, his eyes opening wide before he quickly composes his expression. "Wow, there are no words, Emily. Just… *wow*," he says.

"Ah, thank you?" I reply. "Okay, let's go. I'm so ready for this."

"You know, if you want to run, I can probably hide you really well," Sam offers.

"I'm done running. I've been running from what I want for long enough. It's time to just start taking what I want. The first thing being Josh. So, let's go."

I have no idea why everyone thinks I'd want to run. Have they not met Josh? Any girl would die to be his. And I get to be his. *Forever.* The thought of tying myself down to anyone used to freak me the hell out. But with Josh, I couldn't be more at peace with the idea.

Now that I know I'm not a wanted woman, and

the incident I left behind in Adelaide is not going to come and affect Josh in any negative way, I'm not running anymore. Granted, there is still the issue of the crazy detective stalker to deal with, but I have every faith in Josh that he will find him before the man finds me.

I just wish I knew what he wanted with me. Why me? Shaking all the negative thoughts from my head, I focus on more positive ones, like Josh and how he proposed to me, the song lyrics still playing through my mind. This is what I need to be focused on: Josh, and only Josh.

OKAY, I wasn't nervous… But sitting in a judge's office for the last forty minutes has me a little shaken. Where is he? Why the bloody hell isn't he here? He said he would be here. He has to just be caught in traffic or something.

"Can you try to call him again?" I ask Sam, who is tapping away on his phone in the corner. He picks his head up. Whatever he's about to say gets cut off by Dean.

"I'll call him. There has to be a reasonable explanation for why he's late, Emily. He wouldn't miss this for the world. Trust me, there is nothing Josh wants more in this world than to marry you." Dean walks outside as he places his phone to his ear.

"He will be here. We just have to wait a few more minutes," I tell the judge, who gives me a patronising, sympathetic look.

"Miss Livingston, we can always reschedule. I'll give him ten more minutes. If he isn't here by then, we will reschedule for tomorrow or the next day."

"He will be here. He wouldn't stand me up. He wouldn't do this." I know Josh. I know he wouldn't leave me at the altar, so to speak. He wants this just as much as I do. I know he does. However, that doesn't mean I'm not going to wring his bloody neck for making me wait as soon as I see him.

"Fuck!" Sam curses as he storms out of the office. "Dean, get Emily home now." His voice carries through the open door, and I run towards the sound. He knows something and I want to know what it is.

"Hold the fuck up. What's going on, Sam?" Dean asks, blocking Sam's path to the lift.

"Your idiot fucking brother went rogue, when I clearly told him not to do anything alone. That's what. I need to go and find him, and he better not be already fucking dead."

"W-what do you mean?" I ask, coming up behind him. Sam curses under his breath before he turns around to face me.

"Emily, I'm going to find him, okay? I need you to go home and wait for me there." Sam walks past Dean and stabs at the button for the lift.

"I'm coming with you," Dean says.

"Someone has to get her back to your house, Dean. Get her home. I'll arrange for extra security and I'll text you where I am heading. You can meet me there."

The doors to the lift ping open. Dean looks like he wants to argue more, but he simply nods his head.

"Come on. Ella, call Bray. Tell him he's needed." Dean holds the doors open for us. I look back to the judge, who is now standing in his office doorway. I don't want to leave. Josh said he'd be here.

"Emily, we will come back, okay? As soon as we find him, we will be back here." Dean's voice is soft, although I pick up on his urgency to get me in the lift.

Numb, I'm numb. I want to fight and argue. I want to scream that he will be here, yet I find myself silently walking through the doors and following Dean and Sam's lead.

It's midnight and there's still no sign of Josh. Sam and Dean still haven't returned, although I've heard

Ella on the phone to Dean a few times over the last several hours. All I can do is sit here and wait. Both Ella and Bray keep looking at me like I'm about to break. But they don't know that I'm already broken. I am screaming on the inside.

I can feel something trying to seep out of my pores, something dark. I've never felt like this before. My skin itches and my mind's locked on remembering the pin number Josh entered when he opened his armoury this morning. It's not hard to recall the numbers he used. One, four, one, zero, one, four. It's the date of our first time together.

I'm not sure why my mind is stuck on that room. Something is drawing me towards it though. I think about what Josh would be doing if I were the one out there somewhere. The possibilities of what happened, what could happen, endless… He wouldn't just be sitting here waiting. No, he'd be out there burning down the town until he found me. He wouldn't care how many bodies he left along the way. I just need to know where to start. If I knew where to start, I could come up with a plan. I could go and bring him back myself.

I keep watching the door, waiting for him to walk through. He's going to walk through any minute now and wrap me in his arms. When the doors open, my heart stops as I watch Dean and Sam enter… without Josh. I look behind them but he's not there.

Standing up, I walk over and search down the empty hallway. He's not here. "Where is he?" I ask them, folding my arms around myself.

"Emily, we… ah. We…" Sam attempts. He can't even look at me. I turn to Dean for an answer.

"Emily, we couldn't find him. We found his car parked out front of an abandoned cottage. It's an address Detective Jones was traced to this morning. We searched the house. Josh wasn't there." Dean averts his gaze. Ella slides up to his side and I watch as he wraps an arm around her shoulder.

"You're not telling me something. What aren't you telling me?" I won't be kept in the dark. This isn't something they can protect me from. I need to know. I need to find him.

"There was fresh blood in the entryway of the cottage. We don't know whose it was. All we know is that Josh was there. His car was left there."

"Well, we need to find him. He's out there somewhere and he needs us to find him. We have to find him." I let one tear slip. Swiping at the traitorous thing, I stiffen my spine.

"If you guys can't find him, I will. I'm not going to sit around here and wait. If it were any of you out there, you all know Josh would be the first one on the hunt."

I turn and head towards Josh's room. Now that I know Detective Jones has something to do with it, I know what I need to do. It's not Josh he wants. It's me. My life for Josh's is one I will gladly trade.

"Emily, wait. You have to let us get some more intel. We will find him. I won't give up until we find him. Just give us time." Sam follows me to the bedroom.

"And what if time is something he doesn't have right now? What if he's out there bleeding out somewhere, Sam. I won't lose him. I can't." I slam the door and lock it. I don't want anyone crowding me right now.

Taking out my phone, I open up the Facebook app. Detective Jones still hasn't accepted my friend request. I go through the process of creating a new profile—one using my real name and picture. Once it's set up, I send another friend request to Detective Jones. Clicking on the bubble icon, I type a private message. Please let this work.

Me: You have something I want back. Let's talk. Emily

I put the phone down on the bedside table. Walking into Josh's closet, I pull one of his shirts down, changing out of the white dress, the same one that was meant to hold happy memories. I scrunch it up and throw it into the bin in the corner of the room. I will never wear that again; it should be burned.

I crawl under the covers and lay my head down on Josh's pillow. Inhaling, I can smell him. I know he's still alive. I know he's out there somewhere because if his heart had stopped beating, I would feel that. I would be able to tell. But I can still sense our connection. I've always felt the connection with Josh. Through all those years of torture with Trent, I could still feel Josh's love for me. I cling to my phone, close my eyes and send up a prayer.

In the quiet, dark room, I let myself fall apart. Silent tears stream down my face. In the morning, I will be stronger. In the morning, I will be braver. In the morning, I will find him. And I will bring him home.

CHAPTER 19

JOSH

"Fuck me," I groan as consciousness starts to seep in, my eyes slowly blinking open. Why the fuck does my head hurt so damn much? Raising my hand up towards the pounding in my temples, I'm jerked back as my arm is halted.

My eyes then snap open. What the fuck? My arms are tied down to a chair. Attempting to kick out with my feet, I look down. Motherfucker! Realisation sinks in. I'm trapped. Then, I remember how I got here.

I search the darkness of the room I'm in. I'm alone. But I know that fucker is watching from somewhere. "I'm going to fucking enjoy washing my hands in your blood, you fucking asshole!" My scream echoes off the walls.

Fuck! Emmy's face, a vision of pure innocence, comes to mind. She's going to be bloody pissed that I'm late for what is meant to be our marriage ceremony. I'm going to enjoy slaughtering this fucker even more. He's made me late for my wedding day. *For marrying Emily*. The one thing I've wanted to do since I was sixteen.

Wherever the fuck he is, I'm sure he won't be far. If he thinks he's going to break me, he picked the wrong fucking guy. I'm un-fucking-breakable. Let him bring his worst. I've already met the devil. I was bloody well raised by him. I'm the spawn of Satan himself. I laugh into the empty room.

I wonder just how pissed Emily is going to be about me missing our appointment... I focus on wiggling my toes and fingers slightly, to keep the blood flowing. The last thing I need is to get out of these binds and then not be able to fucking move because my limbs give out on me.

There has to be something around here I can use to get myself out of this mess. I can't see shit. There's a slither of light creeping under what must be the door, but other than that, there's nothing. Pure darkness. The room is cold, but I've been colder. It stinks like mildew. Stale, wet air. What I wouldn't do to bury my head in Emily's hair and get a whiff of that fruity, raspberry scent she always seems to smell like. If I close my eyes and imagine it hard enough, I can almost trick myself into believing that's the scent I'm smelling right now.

I MUST HAVE DOZED OFF, because I come to with a start when I hear the doorknob wiggling around. It's playtime, motherfucker. This is probably going to hurt a little. Pain can be good though; pain means you're alive.

The light that comes on as soon as the door opens blinds me. I have to squint my eyes to see the shadow of the fucker who thinks he'll survive this. I don't need to see him though. I already know who the fuck this dead man walking is.

"Nice of you to finally wake up. I've been waiting. I don't like to be kept waiting. You see, Joshua, when I get bored, I tend to find young, pretty things to keep me occupied. To alleviate the monotony."

My eyes are trained on his face. It's odd… I've never met anyone who's more psychotic than I am. But this dipshit certainly takes the cake. He's as nutty as they come. He pauses his sentence as he hefts on a rope he's dragging behind him.

"This one here is your fault, Joshua. You shouldn't have kept me waiting," he says, kicking the body of a young woman. She lets out a whimper. She's still alive... If he's expecting me to react, he's underestimated me.

I shrug my shoulders up and down the best I can while my arms are fucking tied to a chair. "It seems more like a *you* problem than a *me* problem."

"Oh, you're funny." He drops the rope and walks closer to me, bending down into my face. I smile. This is exactly where I wanted him.

"You should have given her over when I asked. Now, I'm going to enjoy making you watch as I fuck her battered and bruised body. She was promised to me. She belongs to me. Not you," he spits with visible anger.

My head leans back then forward with as much force as I can gather. I hear the crunch of bone as my forehead smashes into his nose. My vision blurs. Fuck, I probably shouldn't have used my head. But seeing the blood currently running out of his nose makes the pain worth it.

"You will never get your hands on her," I growl out.

His fist comes flying at me, connecting with my

jaw. I can't duck or dodge the hit. I just have to sit here and cop it. My head snaps to the side. Spitting on the floor, I straighten my neck and smile at the asshole. I can see I'm already pissing him off. He's only been in the room for two minutes, and I've already managed to fuck with his head.

I look to the girl on the ground. I have no feelings towards her. No empathy. The only thing I can muster is relief. Relief that she's not Emily.

"You know, Emily doesn't even know you exist. Why is it that you think you have a claim to her, exactly?" I've been going out of my mind, trying to figure out what his connection to Emily is.

"I told you. She was promised to me. He was supposed to give her to me. We had a deal. All I want is the girl. So, how about we speed this along, and you tell me where the fuck you have my girl?"

My blood boils at him referring to Emily as his girl. I can't let that shit show. I have to remain calm and unaffected if I want to make it out of here in one piece, and preferably still fucking breathing.

"You might as well go ahead and kill me, because I'll never tell you where she is. You will never get near her." Staring him down, I dare him to make a move closer to me again. He doesn't.

"That's where you're wrong. It's only a matter of

time before she's alone again. You left her at the altar, after all. How long do you think she'll wait for you, huh? Either she's going to walk away and forget you existed. Or she'll come looking for you. Don't worry, I'll punish her regardless of the option she chooses."

He bends down to the girl currently on the floor, curled up in a foetal position. She flinches as his hands reach out and run down her arm. "It's a shame really, such a waste of a good girl. But I was bored, and you were there. You served me well but it's time for you to go." I watch as he pulls out a knife. Bringing it down to where her hands are bound, he slices both of her wrists.

Her screams pierce the air, blood spilling out of her forearms, down over her hands, and pooling on the floor around her. With wide eyes, she looks up at me. I can't help her. There's a slight flicker of helplessness settling within me. Where the fuck that came from, I have no idea.

I clamp that down tight. I don't need now to be the time I start to feel shit I have no business feeling. Instead, I watch, unaffected, as life fades out of her. I don't avoid looking; it's not like I haven't seen a dead body or two before.

The reaction of the detective is disturbing as hell. He's getting off on the fact that he just killed her. I can see it in his heavier breathing, in his dilated pupils. It's fucking sickening.

"You might want to do something about the body. Rigor mortis kicks in after two hours or so, and trust me, disposing of a body after that is not fucking fun."

If I was trying to shock him with my random facts, it worked. His head snaps in my direction, confusion clear on his features.

"Why would I need to get rid of it? She can rot here with you for all I care," he says as he bends down and drags the body over to a corner of the room.

He walks back towards me. I'm preparing myself for the worst. When he stops to retrieve his phone out of his pocket, the sinister smile that spreads across his face does not fucking sit well with me.

"Well, looks like I won't have to get the information out of you after all. My girl has just made contact. She wants to meet me." He turns the phone around and holds it up so I can see the message and profile photo that is unmistakably Emily.

I thought I was prepared for the worst. I wasn't. Why the fuck would she do this? Please, for the love of all that is holy, don't let her be doing this. I start praying right away to a God I don't even believe in.

"Don't worry, I'll be sure to bring her by so you

can say one last farewell." He walks out of the room, leaving me alone.

FUCK! I don't scream out loud. I won't give him the pleasure of knowing just how fucking much I'm panicking right now. Emily cannot come here. My mind is whirling with every possible scenario to explain that message.

Maybe it was Sam. He would do something like that to locate the fucker, then find me. That has to be it. It can't be Emily. We do not end like this. I promised her a future. I promised her memories she could tell her grandkids. These are not the sort I want to give her.

I've been sitting here for what seems like hours. I have no concept of how long it's been. But when the door opens again, my heart stops and all the breath leaves my lungs.

My worst fucking fear—no, my worst fucking nightmare—has just appeared in front of my eyes.

"No! Fuck no! I'm going to fucking kill you, motherfucker. Get your fucking hands off her!" I scream, the rope around my arms and feet burning into my skin as I struggle against it.

"Well, now, that's a reaction I like to see. I believe

you've met my girl—Emily," the cocksucker says as he roughly tugs on Emily's hair, pulling her face up high.

She doesn't let out a sound. She has a blank expression as she stares at me. One side of her face is bruised. This fucker hit her. And I see red.

She mouths the words, "I'm sorry." She's sorry? When I find a way to get us the fuck out of this, you bet your ass she'll be sorry. The lecture I have ready to give her is about keeping what's mine safe and away from psychopaths. Well, psychopaths who aren't me anyway.

Then again, if I can get us out of this mess, I think I'll just hold her tight and never fucking let go. They can pry her body from my cold, dead hands when we're both old and grey and die in our sleep together *Notebook*-style.

"I've waited a long time for you, Emily. You shouldn't have made me wait. Trent promised you'd be mine. Now you are." The detective licks his lips. I want to cut his fucking tongue out of his goddamn head.

"You and I both know Trent was a lying piece of shit," Emily hisses at him. He backhands her across the face, causing her to fall to the ground. She's so close to me. I want to reach out and grab her, to pick her up. Tell her that it's all going to be okay. But it's not. How the fuck am I meant to get us out of this fucking mess when I can't get myself out of this chair?

"I'm going to chop your fingers off one at a time, then I'm going to slice right through your fucking wrist, you sadistic fucking bastard," I seethe at him.

"Words, Joshua, they don't hurt me." He smirks.

"Words might not, but this sure as fuck will." Emily stands up, her own words confident. I'm not the only one who's shocked at what she's doing. The fucking detective's face is priceless. He goes sheet white, staring at her like a stunned mullet.

CHAPTER 20

EMILY

I'm watching the darkened screen, waiting for a reply. My phone beeps with the sound of a notification. My heart pounds as I swipe and unlock the illuminated display. Part of me was hoping it would be a message from Josh, telling me he's on his way home to grovel for missing our appointment with the judge.

Hope's a bitch that's best kept buried though. It's not Josh. It's *him*. The detective. I sit up as I read the message.

Jones: Emily, it's nice to finally hear from you. Meet me at 74 Bourke Street, Newtown. Come

alone. Don't lead anyone here. If you do, I'll kill him before you get to say goodbye.

Shit, okay. *You can do this, Emily*. I'm not the damsel in distress, waiting around to be saved. I'm more than capable of saving Josh. If it means sacrificing myself to do it, then that's a choice I'm more than willing to make. He's going to be pissed as hell at me for doing this. I can hear his voice in my head now, telling me to stop. To go and get Sam or Dean and let them know of the plan.

I can't risk anything happening to him though. If it were me, he wouldn't hesitate to come to my rescue. I owe him that same kind of devotion. Besides, I need to get him back. It's gone beyond a want. It's definitely a need now. My heart is literally hurting without him. My chest is constricted and aching.

With my mind focused on saving Josh, I head into the wardrobe, since Josh has somehow filled it with clothing for me. I choose black leather pants and a long-sleeve black shirt, matching them with a pair of boots. I then chuck my hair up in a messy ponytail.

Now, I just need to figure out how I can get into the armoury and escape this house without anyone noticing. It's the middle of the night; it shouldn't be that hard. Walking down the hall, I stick close to the walls, trying to stay in the shadows, just like Josh had shown me the first night we snuck in here.

My heart hammers in my chest the whole time. I finally come to the door that leads downstairs to where Josh has his armoury stored. It dawns on me I never did get around to asking him why he has so many damn weapons. Although, right now, I'm not complaining.

The adrenaline that is currently running through me is like nothing I've ever experienced. I briefly wonder if this is how my dad would feel when he was deployed. Did he keep going on deployments just to feel this rush?

I close the door behind me and run down the stairs. Punching in the code to the armoury, it opens and the light in the little room automatically springs to life.

I really am spoilt for choice here. There are so many weapons. I'm thankful for those hours spent at the range with Dad. I pick up two small knives, securing one in each of my boots. Next, I need to choose a handgun. Something small I can conceal, yet it has to still pack a punch. If I only get one shot at this asshole, I want to make sure it's lethal.

I select a small, .22 calibre, semi-automatic pistol, tucking it into the waistband of my pants. Just as I'm shutting the door, something stops me. I pick up another small .22. Removing the knife in my left boot, I slip the gun in, making sure my pants sit over the top to conceal it.

I then shut the door, locking it behind me. As I'm climbing the stairs, I send up a little prayer that I can get out of this house without anyone seeing. Shit, what the hell do I do once I'm out? How do I even get to Newtown?

Do I try to take a car? Someone's sure to hear and see that. And there's the whole issue of the gates. I don't know what the code is. There are also guards… As soon as they see me trying to leave, they're bound to call Dean.

I remember the black credit card Josh gave me weeks ago. That will work. I can at least get a cab. Sneaking into Josh's room, I close the door behind me. The tiny hairs on the back of my neck rise. I'm not alone in here.

Turning the light on, I gasp when I see the figure sitting on the sofa. I don't know whether I should turn and run, scream, or see what he wants.

"What are you doing in here, Sam?" I ask as calmly as I can. The fact that I have a few weapons on me gives me more courage than I usually would have in this situation. I'm not helpless right now. I can protect myself. I will protect myself.

"Relax, Emily. I came to check on you. Imagine

my surprise when you weren't here," he says, not making a move to get up, or get out.

"Well, you've seen I'm still here. In one piece. Now, you can leave," I say as I walk over to the dresser. I'm sure I threw that card in one of these drawers.

"I was surprised that you weren't here, but I was more surprised at what I read on this," Sam says, holding up my phone.

Shit, I left that on the bed. My mind was so set on getting down to the armoury I left it behind. I'm not used to carrying a phone around yet. I mostly leave it in the bedroom all the time. How do I get out of this? I'm racking my brain, trying to come up with a reasonable excuse for those messages. But I've got none.

"Have you completely lost your fucking mind, Emily? Because that's the only reason I can think of that would have you trying to sneak out by yourself to meet a goddamn psychopath." Sam stands up and throws the phone back on the bed.

I'm quick to swipe it up, tucking it into my back pocket. "Maybe I am crazy. But I'm not going to sit around here, twiddling my thumbs, when Josh is out there somewhere. He's out there and he's hurt, Sam. I can't just sit back and wait for a miracle, because in my experience, those don't bloody exist. I'm going to go and get him. Then I'm going to wring his damn neck for making me worry like this. I probably have grey hairs by now."

"Emily, you are not going out there. I'll go. I'll find this asshole at the address and I'll bring Josh back."

"No, you can't. You read the message. He'll kill him, Sam. I can't lose him. I only just got him back. You have to let me do this. Please, I can do this. I can."

"What is your plan, exactly, Emily? Charm him with your sweet personality and get him to let both you and Josh go free? That's not going to happen. You don't know the things this sick fuck wants to do to you, Emily. You don't know the risk you're taking here."

"I know. I've seen the pictures. I know what he wants with me. But the risk is worth it to keep Josh safe."

"Just what do you think will happen to Josh if you ended up in one of those pictures, Emily? What do you think would happen to him if he knew the reason you died was because you were trying to save him?"

"He would be alive," I say. I know he'd be a mess. But he'd be breathing, and his friends and family would help him get past it. I have to believe that he would be okay without me.

"No, he wouldn't. You and I both know he's not going to live without you. Fuck."

I dig through the second drawer in the dresser. Finally finding the card, I tuck it into my pocket and head towards the door. Sam beats me to it, blocking my way.

"I can't let you do this, Emily. Please, just let Dean and me handle this," he pleads.

"I tried that. You came home without him, Sam. I won't stop until I get him back."

"We didn't stop. We came to check on you. We came to make a plan, do due diligence."

"Yeah, well, I have a plan and I'm going, so you need to move out of my way." I fold my arms over my chest.

"That's not going to happen. I'm sorry, Emily. I can't let you leave. Josh would have my balls if I did."

Fuck, I have to get out of here. The longer it takes, the more hurt Josh could be. I pull out the pistol from my waistband and aim it at Sam's leg. I don't want to hurt him, but if I have to, I will.

"I won't ask you to move again, Sam. Get out of my way or I will shoot you."

"You're not going to... AH, FUCK! GODDAMN IT, EMILY!"

Sam falls to the ground, holding onto his thigh. His scream is so loud if the gunshot didn't alert the whole household, his shriek alone would have.

"I'm sorry, but I did try to warn you. Also, toughen the hell up. Stop screaming. It's only a flesh wound. I made sure to avoid any major arteries. You'll survive." I step over him and run down the corridor. I can hear him calling after me. I feel terrible for what I just did. But nothing is going to stop me from getting to Josh.

PAYING THE CAB DRIVER, I jump out of the car. With my head held high, I march up to the door and knock loud. My insides churn with nerves, but I'm doing everything I can to not let them show. I will not show weakness. I will be strong. Josh needs me to be strong right now, and I need Josh.

There is no other option. I have to do this. I have to get him back. When the door opens, I realign my shoulders and stare the demon straight in the eyes—eyes, which roam up and down my body slowly, creepiness surrounding his gleam as he takes me in.

This is for Josh. I keep replaying the mantra in my head. It seems like we stand here forever, just staring each other down. I will not be the first to break. I won't speak first. He must not like the defiance I'm putting off because he reaches out and lands a left hook directly to my face. I fall to the ground, my fingers itching to pull out a gun and shoot him. I have to wait. I have to know where Josh is first.

"There's going to be one of those for every day you made me wait, Emily. You were meant to be mine. He promised me you would be mine after four years. That was the deal." He reaches down, grabbing me by the arm, and drags me into the house before slamming the door behind him.

I have no idea what deal he's talking about. Who the hell did he make a deal with? "What deal?" I ask.

"The deal Trent and I made when I signed the fake death certificates for you and your mother. He wanted the money. I wanted you."

"Why?" I question.

"Why? Why do I want you? I've been watching you for a long time, Emily. Trent was never meant to have you first. It was supposed to be me."

"No, why did he want the money? What did he do with it?" Maybe I can find out if there is any of it left, then recover it and give it back to Josh. Not that he seems to care about the cash, but I do. That's a lot of money. If I'd have known he made that account for me, I would have sent it all back to him.

"He owed some nasty people some money. He

never did learn his lesson. Had a bad gambling habit. Always making the same mistakes. But it doesn't matter now, because you're here. You're mine, Emily, and we can start our future together. However short that may be for you, well, that depends on how good you are."

He runs his fingers down my cheek; it takes everything in me not to recoil. I know if I do, he will just get angry again. I can't very well save Josh if I'm in pieces myself.

"What did you do with his body?" I ask. I need to know that Trent's body is never going to be found.

"Oh, you don't need to worry about that, Emily. I helped you. I got rid of the evidence you left behind. Couldn't exactly have you going to jail for murder, now, could I? I put him through a crematorium, then I sprinkled his ashes over the ocean. He always hated the beach." The detective laughs.

"We had a deal. Let me say goodbye to Josh first," I demand. As much as I try to not let my voice quiver, it does, giving away the emotion I'm feeling right now.

"A deal is a deal. And I would so love for him to see that I have you in my grasp now. Let's go." He picks me up, his grip tight around my upper arm as he pulls me through the house.

The moment he opens the door and shoves me

into the room, my eyes go to Josh. The detective grabs me by my ponytail, holding me close to him. I shut all my emotions off. The sight of Josh tied to the chair, the dried blood that's dripped down his face, the bruising I can see… it makes me sick to my stomach.

This is all because of me. He's in this predicament because of me. I mouth the words, "I'm sorry," to him. I need him to know how sorry I am that he's gotten caught up in my mess.

"I've waited a long time for you, Emily. You shouldn't have made me wait. Trent promised you'd be mine. Now you are." Then I see the detective lick his lips as his eyes roam over my chest. It makes me sick.

"You and I both know Trent was a lying piece of shit," I reply to him. It's not until after the words leave my mouth that I realise what I've said. The hand that comes out and slaps me across my face knocks me to the ground.

I can hear Joshua cursing, yelling all sorts of profanity. I need to end this now. With a clear mind and determination, I reach for the pistol in my waistband.

The detective says something about words not hurting him to Josh. He's so focused on Joshua he doesn't notice that I'm now standing and holding a gun aimed at his head.

"Words might not, but this sure as fuck will," I say. I take the slightest bit of pleasure as I watch the shock cross his face.

I don't give him a chance to say anything. I'm not prepared to take the risk of him overpowering me. With my dad's voice in my ear, I focus on the target, breathe, pull my finger back and become one with the pistol.

The sound of the gunshot echoes in the room. The detective's body falls to the ground. I aim the end of the barrel at his fallen form, checking where I actually got him. It's a clean shot, straight in the middle of the forehead. Lowering my weapon, I stare at him, waiting to feel... *something*. Anything. Where's the guilt? The shame? I should feel something other than pure relief right now.

"Emmy, untie me." Josh's hoarse voice breaks me from my inner turmoil.

"I'm sorry... I'm so sorry." Dropping the gun to the ground, I pull out the knife from my boot and cut him loose.

CHAPTER 21

JOSH

Emily pulls a knife from her boot and cuts the rope loose, first from around my ankles and then from my hands. I'm in awe as I watch her. Who the hell is this girl? It's like I am staring at an entirely different person from the one who was scared of her shadow a few weeks ago.

When she walked through that door, I felt sick to my stomach. Seeing her get hit was the worst fucking moment of my life. I know I couldn't watch her get tortured, and that's exactly what that sick fuck had in mind. For her. For me.

As soon as my hands are freed, I pull her into my arms. When she winces, I loosen my hold slightly.

I'm so relieved in this moment, but also pissed as fucking hell that she put herself in this position.

I hear movement in the hall. Shoving Emily behind me, I bend down and swipe her discarded gun from the floor. Dean bursts through the door, followed closely by Zac. I don't lower the firearm. Dean, however, the trusting fool that he is, lowers his. Zac's smarter than I give him credit for because his gun is still trained straight on me.

"What the fuck took you so long? And why in God's name would you let Emily do something so fucking reckless?" I scream at Dean. There's no fucking way I would ever let Ella put herself in danger like Emily just had. I would have locked her in a damn cage if I needed to.

"First, it took a hot fucking minute to track the payment on the card Emily used for the cab she took to get here. Second, I didn't fucking let her out. She snuck out. Ask Emily just what measures she took to get out of the bloody house." Dean smirks, like he knows a secret I don't.

I look behind me and raise my eyebrows at Emily. She rolls her eyes and huffs. "What'd you do, Em?"

"It was only a flesh wound, Josh. It's not a big deal." She folds her arms over her chest.

"Who'd you shoot?" I ask, confused. I'm trying

not to laugh. I shouldn't think it's funny that she shot someone to get to me. But I do.

"Sam, but it was his fault. He wouldn't move out of the doorway. I only shot him in the leg," she defends her actions. She doesn't need to make a case for herself though. Not to me.

"Huh, okay." I turn back to Dean. "Seems like he deserved it."

Dean places himself in front of Zac. "Drop the gun, Josh. You're not going to shoot me."

I tilt my head and stare him down. "Are you sure about that?" I ask him.

"No, but I'd like to think you wouldn't shoot your own brother."

"Okay, well, this little family reunion is great and all, but I'd really like to go home now," Emily says, walking around me. She steps in front of me and takes the gun out of my hand. I'm a little stunned by her boldness so I let her take it.

Cupping her face gently in my palms, I lean in and kiss her forehead. "Let's go home."

"Hey, Zac?" Emily starts in that sugary-sweet voice—a voice I know means that I am going to love whatever it is she is about to say. I've come to know this is the sweet voice she uses when dishing out threats.

"Yeah?" Zac turns around to look at her.

"If you ever point a gun like that at Josh again, I'll shoot your ass before you can even blink. And I don't miss. Just ask the detective back there. Oh, that's right... You can't, because I shot him." Emily smiles. Zac and Dean both stare with slack jaws and wide eyes.

With a shake of his head, Zac says, "I'll take that into consideration, Emily." He turns and continues walking.

"We're going to need a clean-up crew," Dean says before he follows Zac.

"Just torch the place," I suggest as I lead Emily to the Range Rover Zac is currently waiting at.

LYING HERE in bed with Emily in my arms, I finally feel peace again. I honestly wasn't sure if I'd get out of that room alive. Emily's been quiet since I had Zac drop us at my penthouse. With the threat now gone, we don't have to hide anymore. I'm at a loss for words. I'm not sure what to say.

I just know I need to get her talking. She didn't say anything in the car, and she didn't say anything as we showered and climbed into bed. She curled up to my side, wrapped herself around me and clung to my chest, her fingers digging into my arms.

"Thank you. I don't think I said thank you," I say as my hands mindlessly twirl the wet strands of her hair.

"What are you thanking me for?"

"You saved me, Emily. You alone. No help. No one else. Just you. As much as I wish you hadn't put yourself at risk like that, I am thankful that you came to my rescue."

"I would never have stopped looking, Josh. I would have done anything to get you back."

"It's over, Emily. The threat is gone. You are free."

"Josh, do you… do you still want to marry me? I understand if you don't." Emily stares down at the ring on her left hand.

"What? Why would I not want to marry you? Emmy, it's not even a question. We *are* getting married. As soon as I can book an appointment with Judge Thomas, we are signing those papers."

"You're not disgusted at what I've done?" she asks. "Josh, I just killed someone… *again*."

"Emmy, look at me." I tilt her face up towards mine. Once I see those blue eyes, I tell her, "There is nothing you could ever do that would make me not love you. You didn't have a choice. What you did was self-defence, Em. You are perfect in every single way. Never doubt that."

"I should feel bad, guilty, or something. But I

don't. If I had to do it again, I would. And that scares me. Why don't I feel remorse? It's not normal."

"Normal is overrated, babe," I remind her again. "We are exceptional. Normal is for the masses. You're one of a kind. There's nothing wrong with you." I think about what she says. I've never felt remorse in my life, other than when I made her leave town all those years ago. "Emmy, do you think less of me? Are you disgusted by me? You've seen me do unspeakable things. You know I don't feel any kind of remorse afterwards. Fuck, Em, I'd slaughter my whole family if it meant saving you. I would sacrifice anyone. If it were a choice between you and them, there is no choice for me. It's always going to be you."

"I don't know how I got so lucky to have you, but I will always choose you too." Her words mean everything to me.

"You should sleep, babe. It's been a really long fucking day."

"Josh, can we go back to the ranch tomorrow? I mean, if you don't need to be in the city, can we go back?"

"We will head back as soon as we wake up. I promise."

"Thank you."

THREE WEEKS, it's been three weeks since Emily and I returned to the ranch. She was able to reunite with her mum, and honestly, between her mother and mine, I feel like I've hardly got her to myself. Today's going to be different though. Today is the day I get to make her mine. *Legally*. Today is the day I get to call her my wife.

We decided to rebook and have the judge marry us out on the ranch. We've invited just our family and friends. Emily decided that she's friends with Ella's sisters-in-law, which means I have to endure spending time with Ella's brothers, Zac and Bray. I'm getting used to them being around. Would I call them friends of mine? Absolutely not. But they are friends of my brother's, and now apparently friends of Emily's, which means I can't turn the idiots into pig food.

As much as I'd like to think I can hog all of Emily's attention today, I know I'm going to lose her to the girls. I want her to have that moment, to be surrounded by friends and family when she gets ready for her wedding. Even if we're not having a huge ceremony, no expense has been spared.

I let my mother go wild, with the one condition that only family would be in attendance. No press.

No outsiders. She grumbled about how I'm ruining her dreams of a huge wedding, but I reminded her she still gets to do all of that for Dean and Ella, after which she happily arranged everything (happily for the most part anyway).

Wanting to take advantage of the morning, I wake Emily up by burying my head between her legs. This has become my favourite way of waking her. It doesn't take long before she's moaning and squirming underneath me as I slowly swirl my tongue around her clit.

"Shit, Josh, stop. Move." Emily groans as she jumps out of bed and runs to the bathroom.

I follow her, holding her hair back while she prays to the porcelain gods. "Well, that's not the reaction I was hoping for," I say, when she finally stops and leans her back against the wall.

"Oh my God, I'm so sorry. I'm so embarrassed." She covers her mouth with her hands.

Standing up, I fill a glass with water and hand it to her. "Are you okay? Should I call a doctor? Is it nerves?" I really fucking hope she's not getting cold feet.

"I'm fine. I probably just ate something bad. I'm not nervous at all. I get to marry you today. I want to marry you, Josh. Stop worrying." She sips on the water, then bends straight over the bowl again.

"I'm calling a doctor. Hold on." I run out to the bedroom, grab my phone and find the doctor's number that we use in town and dial. It's seven o'clock on a Saturday morning, but I don't care.

"Mr. McKinley, what can I do for you?" Dr. Kapner answers.

"I need a house call, doc. My fiancée is sick."

"What's the problem? When you say sick, what do you mean?"

"She woke up throwing her guts up. It's our wedding day. We're getting married today. I need you to come and check her over." My voice is panicked. The thought of Emily being sick, of something horrible being wrong with her is too much.

"I'm fine. I'm sure it will pass," Emily groans into the toilet.

"Ah, I can be there in about thirty minutes. In the meantime, make sure to keep her fluids up. Does she have a fever?"

I place my hand on her forehead before she bats it away. "No, she doesn't," I answer.

"Okay, that's a good sign. I'll be there as soon as I can. And congratulations on the wedding." He hangs up.

"Fuck, Emmy, what do I do? How can I help?"

"Josh, stop. You can help by not panicking. It's just an upset stomach. That's all. Also, pass me that dressing gown. I'd prefer not to be throwing up into the bowl while I'm naked."

"Shit, yes. Of course." I stand up, retrieve the dressing gown from the hook on the back of the door and help her into it. "Do you want anything? Tea? Coffee? The doctor said to keep you hydrated. You need to drink something."

"Just water is fine. Josh, I'm okay now. Really. I just want to brush my teeth, then lie down for a bit longer."

I pick up her toothbrush and squirt some paste on it. "Open up," I say, holding the toothbrush up to her mouth. She scrunches her eyebrows at me while grabbing the toothbrush.

"I'm going to pretend you did not just want to brush my teeth for me," she says as she stands over the sink.

"You can pretend all you like, but there is nothing I wouldn't do for you, Emmy."

She mumbles a response with the toothbrush still in her mouth. I don't know what it is she said. I just wait for her to be finished. Picking her up, I carry her to the bed and lay her down, getting in next to her.

I send a text to Dean, telling him to direct the doctor up here when he arrives. Putting my phone down, I settle in next to Emily and pull her into my arms. "I can't believe I just threw up when you were doing that," she groans.

I laugh, then Ella comes storming through the door. "What's wrong? Who's sick? Why do you need a doctor?" she demands.

"What the fuck, Ella?" I groan, then I get a look at what she's wearing, or what she's not wearing, which would be clothing. She's walking around in tiny-ass fucking shorts that look more like panties than shorts and a tank top that's fucking see-through.

Rolling out of bed, I storm into the closet, returning with a hoodie. I dump it over her head. "You do know this house is full of staff and you're walking around butt-ass naked, right?" I say as she fights me off.

"Fuck off, Josh. I'm not naked, idiot. Clearly you're not the one who's sick." She ends up taking the hoodie and putting it on. "I'm only wearing this because it's actually cold in here, not because you told me to." She glares at me.

"Whatever you say, sweetheart." I still win, so I don't fucking care about her reasoning. I'm not about to have my household of staff staring at her ass and tits.

"Seriously, Emmy, what's wrong? Why are you sick?" Ella asks her, climbing onto my bed. I pick her up and return her to the floor, jumping back in the bed myself.

"Argh, if it wasn't your wedding day and I didn't think Emily would shoot me, I'd have some not very nice words for you right now, Joshua." Ella folds her arms over her chest.

"I wouldn't shoot you, Ella. I like you. And I'm fine. It's just a tummy bug. I'm sure it will pass," Emily assures her.

Ella's face drops. "Oh God, not you too. Don't get me wrong, I love being an aunt. But you and I were the kid-free people of the group. Damn it, Josh, couldn't you keep it in your pants. Seriously, now all my friends are going to be tied down with babies."

What the fuck is she talking about? Pregnant. Emily isn't pregnant. We would know. Fuck, is she? I look over to Emily, who has also just caught on to what Ella's saying.

"Ah, I'm not pregnant," she says.

Although, judging by the look on Emmy's face, she's not one hundred percent certain of that.

"Ella, can you please go wait for the doctor and let him know which room we are in." I stand up and walk her to the door.

"Fine, but I'll be back. Don't worry, Emily, I'll make you some toast and ginger ale. That always worked for Alyssa and Reilly," she says as I shut and lock the door.

Turning back to the bed, Emily appears terrified. Fuck, I haven't seen this look on her for a few weeks now. She hasn't had any flashbacks; she hasn't been scared of anything. But right now, she looks like she's about to run for her life.

"Emmy, it's okay. It will be okay. When the doctor gets here, we can get him to give us a test. Whatever it says, it will be okay." I'm not sure if I'm trying to reassure her or myself at this point. As much as I want to freak the fuck out right now, I can't. We can't both be freaked out.

"Josh, I'm sorry. I didn't mean to." She has tears running down her face.

CHAPTER 22

EMILY

Pregnant, could I actually be pregnant? How the hell did I let this happen? I swore I'd never let myself get pregnant again… after the last time. I couldn't even protect an unborn baby. How am I meant to be a mother?

"Emmy, this isn't anything you've done wrong. This isn't your fault. Please don't cry. I really fucking hate seeing you cry." Josh wipes the tears from my face. Why isn't he mad?

"I… how? Josh, you don't understand. Last time I was pregnant, I couldn't even protect my unborn baby. How am I meant to be a mother? I don't know how." I verbalize my internal fears.

"Em, you are going to be the most fierce, loyal mother this world has ever seen. What happened last time is not a reflection on you. Just a few weeks ago, look how you were so fearless you put yourself in front of a madman to save me. What do you think you'd do for a child who was ours?"

"I'm scared," I admit to him. I'm so fucking terrified of not being a good mother.

"So am I. We can be scared together. We will learn how to do this together. I promise I will be here every step of the way with you." Josh always says the right thing.

Sometimes I have to pinch myself; his love for me is beyond anything I ever could have imagined. His endless support for what I want, it's like nothing I've ever experienced.

"Are you mad? Angry?" I ask him.

"I'm not angry. I'm not mad, Emmy. I'm… I actually don't know how to explain it. It's a different feeling from anything I've ever felt." He looks contemplative, trying to figure out his emotions.

"What do you feel? Maybe I can help figure it out," I offer.

"I feel like I need to protect someone who I've never met, someone who isn't even here. We don't even know if you are pregnant, Em, but I feel this need, this urge, to not let anything happen to that baby you're growing. Don't hate me, but I'm kind of hopeful that you are. The world could use more people like you in it. And I feel this overwhelming love. You know I love you with every fibre of my being, but this is a different kind of love. I don't know how to explain it." Josh looks down at our joined hands as I rub little circles around his palm with my thumb.

"I think what you're describing is exactly what every parent feels. An unconditional love that knows no bounds. Do you really think we can do this? I mean, I might not be pregnant and we may be worrying about nothing. But if I am, we are going to be okay, right?"

"I have a good feeling that you are, and we are always going to be okay, Emmy."

There's a knock at the door. "Come in." Josh unlocks the door and greets the doctor.

"Mr. McKinley, how's the patient?" An older man with greying hair walks in, carrying a medical bag.

"Thanks for coming, doc. This is Emily. She's better, I think," Josh says.

"I'm fine. He really is overreacting. I'm sorry he wasted your time coming here." I hop off the bed, much to Josh's displeasure, and shake the doctor's outstretched hand.

"I'm Dr. Kapner and I don't mind coming out

here at all. What seems to be the problem?" the doctor asks.

Shit, how do I tell him I need a pregnancy test? Joshua forced the doctor to do a house call for something we could have gotten from the supermarket.

"We need to start with a pregnancy test, doc," Joshua says proudly.

"Emily, is there a chance you could be pregnant?" the doctor directs to me.

I nod my head. I can't look him in the eye. Why am I suddenly so shy?

"Okay, well, let's start with that, and then we can rule out anything else afterwards if need be."

"Okay."

The doctor rummages through his bag and pulls out a box. "Here you go. Just pee on the stick and wait a few minutes," he says, handing the test to me.

"Thank you." I walk into the bathroom. Just as I'm about to turn around, Josh walks in after me, guiding me backwards and shutting the door.

"What are you doing?" I ask him, mortified. He doesn't think he's actually going to watch me pee, does he?

"We are in this together, Emmy. I want to be there for everything. Including the whole peeing on the stick. So, come on, let's do this." He nods his head to the toilet.

"Ah, no. No way. you are not watching me pee, Joshua McKinley." I place my hands on my hips and stomp my foot to get my point across.

"Em, I've literally seen every inch of you naked, licked every curve and crevice. And you're shy about peeing? Really?"

"Yes, so turn around and switch on the tap."

"Okay, you win." Josh places his hands up and pivots on his heel, before running the water in the basin.

I do what I have to do. As soon as the toilet flushes, Josh spins around. "Did it work? Are we pregnant?" he asks eagerly.

I laugh. "You have to wait a few minutes. Put a timer on for three minutes."

We sit there, holding hands on the floor of the bathroom, and wait what has to be the longest three minutes of my life. As soon as the timer goes off, Josh snatches up the stick and turns it over.

"Yes! I knew my swimmers were fucking good," he shouts. I wouldn't be surprised if the whole damn house heard it.

"Oh my God. Josh, it says pregnant."

"Yeah, I can see that. How do you feel?" he asks.

I can't help the tears forming in my eyes. "Surprisingly okay. It's going to be okay. How do *you* feel?" I ask him, noticing his own eyes are shiny with unshed tears.

"I feel like the luckiest fucking bloke in the world. Thank you for giving me this. For giving us this."

"Pretty sure you had a big part of the whole me being pregnant, Josh."

"Yeah, I did. Fuck, Em, we're going to be a family. You, me and this baby." Josh kisses my lips ever so softly before stopping with an abruptness. "Fuck, Emily, you're pregnant. You should not be sitting on the floor. Wait, do you need something? Food? You should probably eat something. Let me call the kitchen. Come on, I'll help you back to bed." He rambles on as we walk out of the bathroom. It's going to be a long bloody nine months, but I wouldn't have it any other way.

"Are you ready to do this?" Josh asks, standing behind me and looking at our reflection in the mirror.

His hands are rested on my stomach, my very flat stomach. I've tried to tell him there won't be anything there to feel for a few months yet, but he's insistent on having his hands there.

As I look at our reflection, I can't believe this day has finally arrived. I'm getting married today, in a fancy white dress and all. This dress is even more beautiful than the first one I had.

It has a lace bodice with long sleeves made out of the softest material I've ever felt. The skirt is silk with a long slit up the front of my left leg. It's gorgeous. But my reflection has nothing on Josh's. He's wearing a tux, a black and white tux. It should be illegal for that man to wear a suit. Just looking at him now, all I can think of is stripping him down and doing very unspeakable things to the body I know he's hiding underneath.

"More than ready."

"Let's do this then. Shall we?" Josh turns and holds his arm out for me. I hook my hand in the loop of his elbow.

We decided to walk down the aisle together. I didn't want anyone to give me away if I couldn't have my dad. Josh's theory was that I already belonged to him, so no one else had a right to give me away.

I'm glad that we are side by side, that I can lean on him as everyone turns and watches us walk down the red carpet.

My eyes take in the beautiful setup Mrs. McKinley has managed to arrange in such a short timeframe. There are two rows of white wooden chairs seated in front of a gazebo, which is covered in pink and white flowers climbing up the sides and arching over the top.

"This looks like something out of a fairy tale, Josh," I whisper.

"Didn't anyone send you the memo, Emmy? You're my queen. A queen deserves only the best."

"If you make me cry and ruin my makeup, I'm going to stomp this stiletto heel into your foot." I laugh. "Thank you for doing this. I couldn't have pictured anything more perfect."

"Even with mascara running down your face, you'd still outshine any fucker here, Em."

We make it to the front. Josh leads me onto the pergola. Now that I'm standing under it, I feel like I'm on a stage. I look back at all of our family and friends. I'm really glad they're here to share this day with us.

My mother is sitting next to Josh's mum. They're both crying, already dabbing their eyes with tissues. Ella and Dean are sitting next to them with Sam on the end, his crutches leaning against the chair. He smiles a huge smile at me. How the guy can even stand being near me after what I did to him, I have no idea. He says that all is forgiven and water under the bridge. But I still feel a little bad for shooting him. I'd do it again though, if it meant getting to Josh.

On the other side of the aisle are Zac and Alyssa. Ash sits between them, his eyes wide and glued to me. I've grown really fond of that kid over the last few weeks. Reilly and Bray occupy the next seats over. Wait, is he? Oh wow, Bray looks like he's trying to discreetly wipe at his eyes. I catch him though; he knows I've seen him do it and he just smiles at me. The couple has one beautiful red-headed little girl on each of their laps. Those twins are bloody adorable, but I pray to God I do not end up with two babies. They're hard work.

Turning my attention back to Josh, the celebrant begins to talk. I get lost in Josh's gaze and it's not until he squeezes my hand to get my attention that I realise I need to focus.

"Joshua, you have your own vows you want to share with Emily?" the celebrant says.

"Emily, from the moment you sat down at my lunch table, I knew you were different. Then you opened your mouth and started rambling on, and I knew you were going to turn my world upside down in the best ways possible. I didn't know or understand the feelings you provoked in me at first, but now I know that was the day I met my soulmate. You make me a better person, Emmy. For so long, I was lost, until you found and completed me. You are my beginning and end. You're the cream to my cookie, the Tam to my Tim, and the toast to my Vegemite. I promise to love, cherish and worship you every day for the rest of our lives." Josh places a solid gold band on my finger.

"Emily, do you have vows you'd like to share with Joshua?" the celebrant asks.

"Joshua, the moment I first saw you, you took my breath away, and still do every time I look at you. I am the luckiest person on earth because I'm loved by you. I promise that you will always be the cookie to my cream, the Tim to my Tam, and the Vegemite to my toast. You are the best part of me. I promise to love you unconditionally for as long as we both shall live." I manage to get through most of what I wanted to say. With tears in my eyes, I slide the ring on his finger.

"I now pronounce you husband and wife. You may kiss your bride."

Joshua has his lips on mine before the celebrant finishes his declaration. His kiss sends a fiery need throughout my body. This is a kiss that I will be telling our grandchildren about, the kind of kiss that inspires love songs. Everything fades into the background as I lose myself in all that is Joshua.

Josh pulls away first. "Are you ready to begin our happily ever after, Mrs. McKinley?"

"More than anything else in the world," I reply.

EPILOGUE

JOSH

2 years later

"Ma-Ma-Ma!" Breanna, my sixteen-month-old daughter, wiggles in my arms, calling out to Emily as we watch her canter on Snow, the new Arabian. She's been out here riding all morning while Breanna and I had a daddy-daughter breakfast date.

I think I wore more of the eggs than Breanna got into her mouth. Then there was the issue of her being covered in syrup. Not that Bree complained about spending half an hour splashing in the bubble bath she then had.

Now, we're sitting on the deck swing. She's trying to jump out of my arms to run towards Emily. I knew from the moment she started moving that Bree was a little daredevil in training. The girl has no bloody fear, no concept of danger. I think I've actually sprouted fucking grey hairs from watching her climb the furniture.

"Isn't Mumma beautiful, Bree-Bree?" I ask, not getting a response other than her chanting, "Ma-Ma."

Turning her in my arms, so she's facing me, I whisper, "I fucking love you, Breanna. Don't ever change for anyone." I know I shouldn't be swearing in front of my toddler, at least that's what her mother and grandmothers keep reminding me. But it's just Bree and me; she's not going to dob me in.

"Dada." Breanna reaches out and pulls on my hair as she lands a very sloppy, open-mouthed kiss to my cheek.

"Did you have a good breakfast?" Emily asks. I was so wrapped up in Breanna I didn't even notice her come up.

"Well, we wore more than we ate, but I think it was good. What do you think, princess? Was breakie good?"

"Ma-Ma." Breanna practically jumps out of my arms as she reaches for Emily.

"Traitor," I tell her when I hand her over.

Emily laughs as she kisses Breanna all over her face. I never knew I was capable of loving something so fiercely, but these two girls are my everything. I can't believe how lucky I am to have them.

Breanna looks just like her mother, absolutely fucking beautiful. I'm sure that shit's going to backfire on me one day, but I'll be ready. I figured I'd buy more pigs when she reaches the age of thirteen. And there's going to be more bodies to fucking bury.

"The Williamsons are coming out this weekend. I've got some workers coming in to set up the yard for the kids."

"What do you mean *set up the yard,* Josh? You've already built a jungle gym. There's a playhouse bigger than most peoples' actual homes, and a bloody petting zoo. What more could you possibly set up?" Emily asks.

When Breanna was born, I may have gone a little overboard building a play yard fit for the princess she is. I'll never admit that to Emily though.

"Emmy, they're only kids once. I have the means to give them memories they can cherish forever. I've booked some theme park rides for the weekend. Who doesn't love a theme park ride?"

"Josh, they can create memories by playing in the dirt. They don't need their own theme park in the back yard. Come on, baby, let's go tidy up your toy room before the kids get here." Emily walks inside the house with Bree in her arms.

"Ah, Emmy, I might have already picked up for her." Emily has this thing about wanting Bree to pick up her toys and pack away after herself.

"Daddy is going to spoil you rotten, little girl." She tickles Bree's belly. "Josh, how do you think she's ever going to learn to pick up after herself if you keep doing it for her?"

"Em, she won't ever have to. I'll always be here to pick up after her." I smile.

"Ah-huh. I'm going to remind you of that when she's sixteen."

"Argh, why, Emmy? Why do you constantly remind me that she's going to be a teenage girl? Are you trying to give me a stroke?" I complain. The thought of my little princess being a teenager is a fucking nightmare.

"Because it's so fun to see the look on your face. Do you remember when I was sixteen, Josh?"

"Of course I do. How could I forget?"

"Do you remember the thoughts you would have about me?"

"No. Just no. Stop right there. This little angel is

going to be a nun. It's already been decided. God wouldn't put such an angelic thing on earth to not have them work for the church." I've already had this discussion with Bray. My girl will be joining his daughters at the convent. We just need to get our wives onboard.

"Yeah, sure. Keep telling yourself that." Emily laughs.

EMILY

Fourteen years later.

"ARGH, I HATE YOU!" Breanna slams the door on Josh's face.

"No, you don't!" he yells back. She opens the door, her arms folded under her chest.

"Every girl my age wears dresses like this. It's not fair that you're making me change."

"Every other girl your age isn't my daughter. I don't care what they wear. What *you* wear, on the other hand, I very much care about that."

I watch the back and forth between the two. It won't be long before Bree wins, and Josh gives in to her. He always does. He can never say no to her.

"I'm not going then. I'll stay home. I'll just stay in this room for the rest of my life, and be the old spinster that still lives with her parents when she's forty."

Josh tilts his head at her and smiles. "Is that meant to be a threat, princess? Because it sounds like a fucking great idea to me."

"Argh, you're impossible. Mum, tell him there's nothing wrong with the dress," Bree pleads. Oh crap, I was really hoping to stay out of this.

Josh turns to me. "Not you too, Emmy. Really?"

he says, looking me up and down.

"You're overreacting, Josh. It's just a dress," I try to reason with him.

"Babe, that may be just a dress, but on you, it's a fucking wet dream."

"Ew, gross. I do not want to hear that," our girl interjects.

"Where do you think you came from, Bree? It wasn't the stalk." Josh laughs.

"Lalalala." She covers her ears.

"Come on, we're going to be late. It's not fair to Ash if we're late because you're being the fashion police."

"Fine, but if any fucker looks at either of you the wrong way, the pigs are getting fed."

"Again, gross. Besides, there's only one guy I want looking at me the wrong way. But you don't need to worry, Daddy. He doesn't even know I exist." Bree walks past us both, leaving us speechless.

"Whoever that boy is, he's a fucking idiot, Breanna," Josh calls to her back.

I have a feeling I know just who that boy is, and he's not really much of a boy at all. He's six years older than her. Let's hope, for his sake, he continues to not notice her, because if he does take an interest in my daughter, he won't have to worry about Josh. He'll have me to deal with.

ASH

It's my twenty-second birthday. I tried to tell my mother I didn't need a fucking fancy dinner party or any big deal made. She ignored me and went ahead and arranged one anyway. I'm now forced to sit at the table all night with my cousins, aunts, uncles, and *her*.

Breanna. She's my cousin's cousin. I know, messy. I've grown up with her. I remember when she was born. I remember when she started talking.

What I don't remember is when she stopped being a little kid who was like a cousin to me, and became the most beautiful girl in the room. And I don't remember when I stopped looking at her like a friend, and started looking at her like she was mine.

She's sitting across from me, wearing a little black dress that leaves nothing to the imagination. I'm not sure how she managed to get out of the house dressed like this. Why the fuck didn't Josh stop her? Doesn't he realise every fucking guy with a cock is staring at her, undressing her with their eyes?

Fuck me, I need to stop. She's sixteen. She's still in bloody high school. I can't think of her like this. Adjusting myself in my seat, I turn and listen to Lily chatting about some party she went to the other night. Or at least I pretend to listen. I have to tune

Breanna out, for both of our sakes. At least for a few more years.

BREANNA

I want to strangle the waitress who keeps batting her eyelashes at Ash. I also want to stab him in the face. In that tanned, sculpted, beautiful bloody face. He hasn't acknowledged me all night.

I dressed up in the hopes he would notice me. I thought maybe tonight would be the night he'd stop seeing me as a little kid. *He did notice*. I saw the little tell-tale signs he was checking me out. But just as quickly as he started to drag his eyes down the silhouette of my dress, he stopped and redirected his attention to Lily.

I see my friend Ben from school over at one of the other tables. Excusing myself, I go and sit next to Ben.

"Fancy seeing you here," I say.

"Beebee, what the hell are you wearing?" he asks as he looks me over from head to toe. He's the only one who gets away with giving me a nickname like Beebee. He started it the day I got stung by a bee when we were in the fifth grade and I swelled up like a balloon.

"It's a dress, Ben. People wear them." I slump down in my chair.

He looks over my shoulder to the table I just left. "He hasn't noticed, huh?" Ben observes.

"Not a word. He just pretended like I wasn't at the table." I think I'm over it now. I'm going to just find a nice boy my own age and start dating. I'm not waiting around for someone who doesn't want me.

Ben wraps his arm around my shoulder. Glancing back towards Ash, he whispers in my ear, "Don't be so sure he doesn't notice, Beebee. Right now, he's looking at me like he wants to tear me limb from limb." He kisses the top of my head and I snuggle into his shoulder.

"Thanks, Ben."

"Bree. Ben, it's great to see you again, but Bree is at a family dinner and needs to return to the table." Oh my god, can my dad be any more embarrassing right now?

"No worries, Mr. McKinley. BeeBee, you look amazing. Don't worry about what anyone else says. *Or doesn't say*," Ben offers as I stand up.

Dad puts his arm around my shoulder. "Is Ben the boy who doesn't notice you exist?" he asks.

"Ew, Daddy. God no. Ben's my best friend—that's all."

"That's good. It'd be a shame to have to make him disappear."

As I take my seat back at the table, Ash glares at me. "Problem?" I ask him, folding my arms over my chest. I don't miss his reaction. His eyes travel to my chest and back up. Maybe he's not so immune to me after all.

"Yes, there is. A huge one," he says before looking away again.

ACKNOWLEDGMENTS

I am thankful first to you, the reader, the one for whom this story was written. And I hope that you enjoyed Josh and Emily's story as much as I have.

Josh and Emily have taken me on an emotional rollercoaster. I cried, laughed and cursed them all in the same day. Their story truly touched my heart.

I am thankful for the support of my family. My wonderful husband, whose support and endless encouragement never fails. Nate, I could not have accomplished this without you.

I want to thank my beta readers. Natasha, Amy and Sam, you girls are one of a kind. Thank you for all of the time and effort you put into reading and providing insightful feedback for *Ruining Him*.

I am ever grateful to Danni Giddings, who wrote and composed the theme song for Josh and Emily.

"Ruining Me" has been playing on repeat while I wrote and edited *Ruining Him*.

The Kylie Kent Street Team, what can I say? I would literally be nowhere if it weren't for you. I often get asked by other authors how I managed to form my street team. My answer is always the same, one hundred percent pure luck, and I'm not ever giving them back!! I believe I have the BEST street team in the business. Not only do you all ARC read for me, but you all read, promote and share whatever I put in front of you so enthusiastically and with genuine interest and excitement. I freaking love you guys!

Thank you, Kat, my amazing editor, who endures my constant messages and rants about these characters. Without you, this book would not be as great as it is now!

ABOUT THE AUTHOR

About Kylie Kent

Kylie made the leap from kindergarten teacher to romance author, living out her dream to deliver sexy, always and forever romances. She loves a happily ever after story with tons of built-in steam.

She currently resides in Sydney, Australia and when she is not dreaming up the latest romance, she can be found spending time with her three children and her husband of twenty years, her very own real life instant-love.

Kylie loves to hear from her readers; you can reach her at: author.kylie.kent@gmail.com

Let's stay in touch, come and hang out in my readers group on Facebook, and follow me on instagram.

Made in United States
Orlando, FL
21 June 2024